Forbidden Fantasy

It hadn't troubled him that a woman was supervising the construction project. In his culture, women took charge as a matter of course. It *had* disturbed him when he realized he'd begun to fantasize about her, but he continued to indulge himself. He wondered about the shape of the legs she hid under her jumpsuits. He knew those heavy work boots must house slender ankles and small, feminine toes.

He knew other women, of course. The difference was that Megan was unobtainable, which made it safe to think about her, even if unwise. He'd come to grips with that earlier, when *she'd* watched *him* work. At first she'd seen him through the eyes of an engineer. But she'd lingered, and he'd felt the scrutiny of a woman's eyes.

He wondered what she'd seen when she looked at him that way.

Dear Reader,

When two people fall in love, the world is suddenly new and exciting, and it's that same excitement we bring to you in Silhouette Intimate Moments. These are stories with scope, with grandeur. The characters lead the lives we all dream of, and everything they do reflects the wonder of being in love.

Longer and more sensuous than most romances, Silhouette Intimate Moments novels take you away from everyday life and let you share the magic of love. Adventure, glamour, drama, even suspense—these are the passwords that let you into a world where love has a power beyond the ordinary, where the best authors in the field today create stories of love and commitment that will stay with you always.

In coming months look for novels by your favorite authors: Maura Seger, Parris Afton Bonds, Linda Howard and Nora Roberts, to name just a few. And whenever you buy books, look for all the Silhouette Intimate Moments, love stories *for* today's women *by* today's women.

Leslie J. Wainger
Senior Editor
Silhouette Books

Kathleen Eagle

But That Was Yesterday

Silhouette Intimate Moments

Published by Silhouette Books New York

America's Publisher of Contemporary Romance

SILHOUETTE BOOKS
300 East 42nd St., New York, N.Y. 10017

ISBN: 0-373-07257-0

First Silhouette Books printing October 1988

Printed in the U.S.A.

Books by Kathleen Eagle

Silhouette Special Edition

Someday Soon #204
A Class Act #274
Georgia Nights #304
Something Worth Keeping #359
Carved in Stone #396
Candles in the Night #437

Silhouette Intimate Moments

For Old Times' Sake #148
More Than a Miracle #242
But That Was Yesterday #257

KATHLEEN EAGLE

is a transplant from Massachusetts to her favorite regional setting, the Dakota prairie. As educator, wife, mother and writer, she believes that a woman's place is wherever she's needed—and anywhere she needs to be.

For Clyde,
Because I love him.

Prologue

Sage Parker hated being locked up. He clenched his teeth when he heard the steel door clank shut behind his back. More than one judge had said that just the sound was enough to convince a man to mend his ways. It was a sound that chilled the blood, all right. That sound combined with the taste of stale cigarette smoke and the smell of dirty socks to start his gut churning. But neither the sound nor any part of this place had ever convinced him to do anything.

Sage glanced over his shoulder at the man in uniform, who jangled the keys on the big key ring and jerked his chin toward the cot near the far wall. "He's got ten minutes before he goes to court, Sage. You know the routine."

Sage knew it well. He nodded as he shoved his hands into the pockets of jeans faded honestly through years of wear. No matter how many times he'd been here, no matter what the circumstances, it never got any easier. He dragged his boot heels against the cement floor as he approached the cot.

"How're you doing, Jackie?"

The man sitting on the cot had heard the sound of the cell door, too, but he hadn't looked up. He hung his head and stared at the patch of floor between his feet as he hugged himself around the middle. The question went unanswered.

Sage looked down at the top of the man's head and struggled against the urge to turn around and walk out. This was the drunk he most hated seeing—the one who had fallen off the wagon after a period of sobriety. It disgusted him first, but he recognized that feeling as a cover-up. Truly, it scared the hell out of him. Finally, it humbled him. He laid a hand on Jackie's shoulder and sat beside him on the cot.

"Got the shakes, huh?" Jackie didn't have to answer that question, either. Sage felt the man's tremors under his hand. The tribal judge would commit Jackie to a detoxification program, but shock was an imminent danger now. "Are you going to make it, Jackie?"

Jackie shook his head slowly. "I dunno, Sage. I dunno. I don't feel too good. I just dunno." The litany became a hoarse whisper.

Sage acknowledged the watchful eye of the closed-circuit camera. The officer at the front desk had seen the bulge of the two ounce bottle Sage carried in his breast pocket when he made calls like this. Nothing had been said. There was a tacit understanding that

Sage Parker knew what he was doing. He drew a deep breath and exhaled slowly.

"You think a shot would straighten you out enough to get you to detox?"

Jackie turned his head and let Sage see the hope those words had sparked in bleary, blood-shot eyes. Sage scorned that false hope, but he couldn't help sympathizing with the man for being sucked in by it. He pulled the airline-size bottle from his breast pocket and broke the seal. It was a good brand, Sage thought, but then, he'd always bought the best when he was buying. He tipped the bottle to Jackie's lips and administered the gin carefully, as though it were a dose of medicine. Jackie reached up, but Sage held the bottle tightly, pulling it away as Jackie swallowed.

"Thanks." Jackie wiped his mouth with the back of a shaky hand. "The rest of that's just gonna go to waste, Sage."

"Yeah, well..." Sage lifted a shoulder as he capped the bottle. "Better to waste the gin than get wasted ourselves." He slipped the bottle back into his pocket and gripped Jackie's shoulder again. "Right, friend?" Jackie nodded dumbly. "You'll stop shaking in a minute."

"For a while, at least."

"Yes," Sage said quietly. "For a while."

The keys rattled in the lock again, and both men looked up. "Time to face the music, Jackie," a police officer announced.

Sage helped Jackie to his feet. The handcuffs were always the worst part, he thought. The clicking sound pinched his heart.

"Think he'll be okay for an hour or so?" the officer asked Sage.

"He won't make it through any lectures from the judge."

"You've heard 'em all, anyway," said the policeman with a laugh. "Haven't you, Jackie?"

Jackie ignored the question as he cast a soulful look over his shoulder. "I'm sorry, Sage. I met up with some old buddies, and I thought I could handle it. Six months down the tubes now, huh?"

"You'll start over." Sage gave a nod toward the open door. "First things first, Jackie. We'll be waiting for you."

"I was doin' good, though, wasn't I?"

"You were doing great."

Jackie squared his shoulders and crossed the threshold with his escort. "See? I was doin' great."

"You weren't doing so great when they picked you up last night," the officer reminded him.

Sage was glad to walk out of the cell. He put his hand over his breast pocket as he watched the man in uniform lead Jackie down the hall. He could feel the heat of the liquid burning his hand through the glass and the cotton cloth. No matter how vehemently he denied it, there was a distant longing out of the past that nagged at the weaker part of his brain. He gave the men's room door a hard shove and strode to the sink to pour the rest of the stuff out. He never carried a bottle with a broken seal, and he never tossed a bottle for someone else to find. He even rinsed it out before he dropped it in the trash can. If he'd left any "corners," it was only water, which couldn't hurt anybody. Sage was thorough. He had to be. He was responsible for his own actions, and he had the weaker part of his brain to consider.

Chapter 1

Sun-bronzed and bare to the waist, the man wielding the jackhammer was an arresting sight. His flesh vibrated as though charged by the power he held in his grip. A red bandanna kept the sweat out of his eyes, but his body was beaded with it, and the moisture glistened in the South Dakota sun like the mica in a granite road cut. Small beads gathered in the central valley of his chest to form a rivulet, which made a quick run to his abdominal plane and disappeared into his jeans.

Megan's gaze skittered over the power tool that was framed by the man's flexed-knee stance. Its bit gouged without mercy at the face of rockbed that had been gauged, sampled and declared by Megan McBride to be in the way of progress. She wondered how this man felt about changing the face of the earth. After all, he was an Indian—Native American, she amended mentally—and traditionally they resented the kinds of changes she was in the business of making. Perhaps it didn't offend him too much. He was doing his job and doing it well. If he had any sense that he was being watched, he gave no indication of it as he concentrated on his work.

"Sage Parker." Megan jumped at the words shouted close to her ear. She turned a questioning look at the older man who stood behind her shoulder. Didn't Bob think she knew the names of the men on her crew by now? "Good man," Bob added. "Let's go back to the trailer where we can talk."

The noise level wouldn't be much better in Megan's mobile office, but at least it would be possible to talk there. The machine-gun rattle of the jackhammer became distant as they made their way down a steep grade, turning their feet sideways to keep from sliding. Bob Krueger was a gentleman of the old school, prepared to offer Megan a hand despite the fact that her young body handled this activity far more gracefully than his older one did, but he curbed the impulse. The old school wouldn't have allowed a woman on a road construction site, certainly not as the engineer in charge of the project. Offering her a hand in front of her all-male crew would have been a disservice.

Megan noted the progress of the big yellow earth movers. She knew the operators would be watching one another, each challenging himself to move more dirt than the other. It was a form of competition that kept an otherwise tedious job interesting. They would blast through more rock before the day was out, and, if all went well, they would remain on schedule.

"How're you getting along with Taylor?" Bob offered the question after they'd closed the trailer door and left at least a portion of the dust outside.

Megan eyed her foreman's desk. He wasn't much of a record-keeper, and the desk showed little sign of organized use. "So far, so good," she said. "But, in his mind, I think the project is yours, and I'm just a messenger."

Bob sat on the corner of Megan's desk, which was clear of all but two file folders and a clipboard. She was careful to protect her work from the fine dust that was always in the air on a construction site.

"Has he challenged your authority in any way?" Bob asked. He was a veteran of the Highway Department and a man with enough experience to know that skill, not gender, was the measure of a good highway engineer.

"Not yet," Megan said as she pulled out a file drawer. "But I think he'd like to. Whenever we talk, I get the feeling there's one more thing he wants to say, but he decides he hasn't quite got me figured out well enough to risk it."

"Are you ready with a response?"

She withdrew a folder and gave the older man a smile that lent a hint of feminine sophistication to her startlingly blue eyes. "How long have you known me, Bob?"

"Since you started with the highway department. What was it? Five—six years ago?"

"Eight, if you count my summers on the survey crew." She raised an eyebrow as she slid the drawer shut. "I'll admit I didn't always have a ready response in those days, but I've made a habit of updating my repertoire."

"Loaded with classics, I'm sure."

Megan laughed. "Whatever brings the most respect. With these guys, that's likely to be honky-tonk rather than classical."

Bob nodded as Megan handed him the folder. He flipped it open. "Anyone else causing you any problems?" She was his protégé, and he wanted this project to go well almost as much as she did.

"Not really. Not…seriously." Bob glanced up from the first page of the report she'd handed him and waited for her follow-up. She folded her arms and rested the backs of her thighs against the edge of the desk. "A couple of the men seem to have trouble getting themselves to work sometimes."

"Transportation problems?"

She lifted her shoulder. "They've offered that as an excuse once or twice."

"Are they buddies with Taylor or something?"

Megan chortled. "Hardly."

"It doesn't matter. A lot of guys are looking for work, Megan. Don't put up with any—"

"Taylor would like to fire them, but—" The look in her eyes told him how uncomfortable she was with the problem. "We had very few applications from Native Americans, and I don't want to fire the ones we've got. They're good workers, but there are two men—well, one in particular—"

"Not Parker, I hope."

Megan shook her head quickly. "No, Parker's completely reliable."

Bob smiled, apparently relieved by the news. "Parker's the best man on your crew. I'd hate to hear he wasn't making it to work."

Visions of the man flashed through Megan's mind. She'd learned that he could handle almost any job on the site, from heavy equipment to explosives. In her business she saw brawny, sweaty men all the time. It was Sage Parker's versatility that caught her attention, not his virility. Reliability, versatility—those attributes should not go unnoticed.

"So why don't you see if he can help you with the others?"

The question reclaimed Megan's attention. "Who? Parker?"

"If you're not ready to fire these guys, you might get some ideas on how to handle them from Parker. I hear he's got some kind of recovery program going on the reservation."

"Recovery program?" She pronounced the words as though they were part of a foreign tongue.

"For alcoholism."

"Nobody said these men had a drinking problem, and I'm not jumping to any conclusions just because—"

"Of course you're not," Bob said calmly. "Neither am I. I'm suggesting you let Parker in on your concern and see what he's got to say. I've worked with him off and on over the years. He's put down a lot of miles."

"You don't think he'd . . . take offense?"

"You're the boss here, Megan. And you're the only woman." Bob nodded toward the door and offered a conspiratorial grin. "To a man, those guys are all worried about offending *you*."

Whenever Karl Taylor went to the office there were bets taken. One of these days he was bound to make the same kind of remark to McBride's face as he made behind her back, and one of them was going to come flying out the door. Some said the lady would flee in tears. Others thought she'd kick Taylor out on his butt. Either way, the crew enjoyed the suspense. They were disappointed once again when Taylor emerged at quitting time and closed the door behind him.

"Hey, it's time to knock off for the day!" he announced. "What's everybody standing around here for? How about a stop at the Red Rooster?"

Sage only half-listened as he buttoned his shirt, calculating the distance between himself and a shower. He tossed his leather work gloves on the seat of the pickup and dug in his pocket for his keys. He lifted the corner of his mouth in a smile as he noticed the way the stiffened gloves had landed, with the fingers curled and clawing at the air. Great for a movie, he thought. *Ravaging Gloves*.

"Hey, Sage." Sage turned his head toward the hand on his shoulder, then looked up at Scott Allen's friendly, sunburned face. "Come on over to the Rooster with us. I'll stand you a game of pool."

"Some other time, Scott. I've got horses standing around a dry stock tank right about now."

"Gotta take some time off once in a while." Scott gave Sage an amicable parting pat on the shoulder. "You work too hard, buddy."

"Making up for lost time," was the reply Sage regularly gave to that comment, although he knew few people really understood what it meant.

"Parker!" Taylor's voice brought Sage around again, this time more slowly. He needed the extra seconds to prepare his patience. "Boss lady wants to see you before you take off." Taylor snatched off his cap and wiped his forehead with his sleeve. He chuckled as he put it back on and adjusted the bill. "Ain't that a crock? My wife's the only 'boss lady' I ever expected to answer to, and there's no way in hell she'd take on a job like this."

"Thought you said your wife used to flag," one of the men reminded him.

"Way back when. Now she's home raising kids."

Sage stuffed his shirttails into his jeans and slammed his pickup door. He'd heard enough of Taylor's "wisdom" on women. He wanted to tell the ruddy-faced foreman that spouting that nonsense on this particular job was a sure sign of his incompetence, but Sage needed the work. The fact that the engineer on the project was a woman didn't bother him. Being summoned to the boss's office was another matter.

"Hey, Sage, why don't you stop in for something cold to drink?" another man asked as he walked by.

"I already asked him, Randy. He's gotta get home."

Sage offered the two young men a smile and lifted a forefinger as he walked past their pickup. "You have one for me, Randy. Just one."

"The legend lives on," Scott teased. "You entered up in the bronc riding this weekend, Sage? I'd like to have a chance to beat you out, just once."

Sage laughed. "You wish! The legend lives on because I know when to quit. You guys take it easy."

Sage lifted the bandanna from his head and raked his fingers through his hair as he wadded the cloth and stuck it in his back pocket. The metal steps wobbled under his work boots as he took a deep breath and reached for the doorknob. He'd turned this summons over in his mind several times, and he couldn't come up with a reason for it. He'd been doing his job. He'd done every task Taylor had tossed at him, and he'd never been late for work. But experience told him that being called to the office generally meant he was about to be reprimanded, and he'd never handled that well.

When she looked up from the chart on her desk and smiled, his first thought was, Don't do that lady. It makes you look too damn cute. "Taylor said you wanted to see me."

"Yes. I know it's time to go home, and I promise not to keep you long." She rose from her chair and moved to the front of the desk.

Sage stood about as close now as he'd ever been to her, and it occurred to him that he hadn't really noticed how small she was. She wore her honey-blond hair cropped short in back and styled longer on top. He detected little makeup, and the clarity in those deep blue eyes made him uneasy. It wasn't a look he could deal with. There was nothing hazy, or frosty or even provocative about it. Her eyes were simply bright and clear.

"Bob Krueger was here today. He's pleased with our progress." She folded her arms and leaned back against the desk. There was nothing feminine about her khaki jumpsuit—except, perhaps, for the way she had the collar turned up in the back—or her lace-up work boots, besides the fact that they were the smallest pair he'd ever seen. Sage shoved his hands in his pockets and waited for her to come to the point. "He had high praise for you."

But? "I've worked on a few of Bob's projects."

"So he said. You seem to be trained for every job on the site."

"I've had a lot of years' experience in highway construction." She'd read his application. She knew that.

"Are you an engineer, too?"

He returned her level gaze. "I've had some vocational training, but I've never been to college." He jerked his chin toward a cabinet. "That's all in your files. Somebody decided I was qualified for this job, and they hired me."

"I think you're *overqualified*, Sage. You should have applied for foreman."

Sage scowled. What was this all about, anyway? "We've got a foreman on this project, and you're the engineer. My paycheck's the same whether I set charges or operate a blade."

"I just want you to know the opportunity's there the next time you apply. Bob thinks very highly of you."

Sage drew his hands out of his pockets slowly as he struggled to fit the pieces of this conversation together. That clarity he'd seen in her eyes might have been misleading. "Am I being fired from *this* project, or what?"

"Of course not. I just wanted to pass Bob's compliment on to the person who should hear it, and then I—" She raised her eyebrows in a kind of confession. "I wanted to ask for a favor."

"A favor?"

She braced her hands on the desk at either side of her hips. The suit she wore gave no hint of the shape of those hips, but the crisp cotton fabric had stretched across her thighs when she leaned back. It wasn't the first time he'd caught himself wondering about those thighs.

"Advice, really," she said. "I don't know what to do about Jackie Flying Elk. He hasn't been to work for two days, and Karl wants to fire him."

Sage drew a long breath and released it slowly. He had to remind himself that, yes, Jackie was his business. He'd taken four hours' leave on Jackie's account. But the man was responsible for his own job. This woman had called him in here to talk about one of her employees just because he was Indian.

When Sage made no comment, Megan continued. "Jackie is very good at his job, and I don't want to fire him. I'd like to give him another chance. He's got to get back here tomorrow or have a good excuse, Sage. I can't—"

"Why are you telling me this?"

"Well—" She knew it was a good question, and she wasn't sure she had a good answer. "I can't find a phone number for him."

"He doesn't have a phone. I can tell you where he lives." He saw the reluctance in her eyes, and he knew then that he hadn't been wrong about them. They hid nothing.

"I thought maybe you could talk to him. You're friends, aren't you?"

"Of course. Jackie Flying Elk, Gary Little Bird, Lawrence Archambault. Who else have you got? We're all buddies. I even get along with some of the white guys on the crew."

Megan pushed her fingers through her hair and cast a glance at the ceiling. "I'm going about this all wrong." She braced her hands against the desk again. "I was hoping you'd talk to Jackie. Tell him to come back to work tomorrow. I don't know what else to do."

"If Jackie's run out of chances, you do what you have to."

"I'm trying to be fair." Cornered, Megan always bristled like a cat. She knew she was doing it now, and she made a conscious effort to control her voice. "I've wondered . . . it's possible that Jackie has a drinking problem, and if he does—"

"It's also possible that *I* have a drinking problem."

"If you do, it doesn't interfere with your work." Her fur was up again. "In Jackie's case, it will mean the loss of his job. He's definitely letting it get out of hand if it's . . . if it's what I think it is."

"You're very perceptive, Miss McBride. It does sound like Jackie might have a problem." Sage was beginning to enjoy this conversation. She was every bit as uncomfortable now as he'd been when he'd first come through the door. "I can't solve it for him."

"All I'm asking you to do," she said carefully, "is *talk* to him. Tell him to be here at eight tomorrow morning."

"Jackie won't make it to work tomorrow, and no amount of talk is going to change that."

Megan's shoulders sagged, and she looked as though he'd just surprised her with a totally unexpected checkmate. "Why not?"

"Because he's sick, Miss McBride."

"Why didn't you tell me that in the first place? If he's sick—"

"He *was* drunk. Now he's sick. It takes a while to dry out."

She should have kept the desk between them, Megan decided. He was standing there telling her things that somehow scared her, and there was no emotion whatever in his dark eyes. If she had her desk and her charts and her aerial photographs spread out between them, she would feel stronger. She thought of Jackie, who worked like a beaver and kept the crew laughing at his jokes. "Is he in . . . jail?"

"He's in a detoxification unit."

She wasn't sure what that meant, but she nodded. "Could we call that a hospital?"

"You can call it whatever you want. It's staffed by medical people."

"Would they be able to give me any indication—"

"Look, you're not gonna know what they can tell you unless you call and ask." He lifted one corner of his mouth in a humorless smile. "You don't have to risk actually setting foot on Pine Ridge soil, Miss McBride. The detox unit has a phone."

"I have been to Pine Ridge," she said patiently. "Please understand that Jackie's problem bears no reflection on the Native American members of our crew. Anyone who misses work without calling in gets a warning, a reprimand, and then—"

"And then he gets fired. If you have a policy, why aren't you sticking to it?"

Megan came away from the desk and took a stance that said she might be willing to square off with this man, despite his size, in defense of the poor man she'd hoped Sage would defend.

"I believe the circumstances might be mitigating," she said.

"In what way?"

"He—" Pick something, she told herself. "You said yourself that Jackie doesn't have a phone."

"So I did."

"And you said he was sick."

He'd said it once. No confirmation was necessary.

"Illness is a valid excuse for missing work."

"So there you have it." He appeared to toss the issue off with a casual shrug. "Your problem is solved."

"But for how long?"

"Good question." Sage had been standing over a jackhammer most of the day. He decided Taylor owed him a seat, so he sat on the foreman's desk. "What are you going to do about Gary Little Bird?"

"He's not as bad. He's had a warning."

"You must have forgiven the day he came to work an hour late."

"He had car trouble."

"Did he?" He folded his arms across his chest. "Did you know that before this weekend, Jackie hadn't had a drink in six months?"

"But he's—"

"Missed work. I know. Because he drives an Indian car." He lifted one shoulder. "Or should I say *Native American*? Probably came out of Detroit. We buy American made, American used. Before the summer's over, my pickup will be sitting along the road halfway between my place and here, and I'll be tinkering under the hood for most of the morning. It's heated up on me twice in the last week."

"If that happens—"

"You'll dock me. That's the policy." He stood up and tucked his thumbs in the pockets of his jeans. "Look, Miss McBride, I'm sure you mean well. You know, by rights it's Taylor who runs the crew. I'll do what I can for Jackie, but that doesn't include taking care of him on the job. I suggest you make that call and talk to the doctor."

On impulse, Megan offered a handshake. "Thank you for your time, Sage. I've learned a great deal." Her hand disappeared in his, but he was captivated, too—by her eyes. "Bob Krueger *did* say you were the best man I had on this crew. I thought you should know that."

Sage nodded, released her hand and turned to leave without another word. She was a bit stunned when he shut the door behind him.

* * *

His family had lived on the western side of Pine Ridge Indian Reservation for at least four generations. Before that, they had been part of the nomadic band of Lakota people known as the Oglala. They were not related to the Commanche Parkers, but he was often asked if the famous Quannah Parker had been an ancestor. So far as he knew, he had no famous ancestors. His great-grandmother had married a mixed-blood named Parker, who had given her his name and his child and then wandered away.

Sage turned his battered blue pickup at the approach to his part of Parker land and drove between the two huge posts that had been set there in better days. The crossbar had fallen some time ago. Sage had set a goal for himself. When he owned a hundred head outright, he would put up another crossbar and hang a sign. With a hundred head of cattle, he could call this a ranch again.

His place bordered some of the most scenic land east of the Black Hills—the South Dakota Badlands. The government had once ceded all this land to the Lakota, including the Black Hills, but gold had been discovered, and the Hills had been seized once white occupation had become an accomplished fact. The Lakota had been assigned to various Dakota Territory reservations, which shrank in size over the years. The Oglala had been given this site within teasing reach of the sacred Hills. The Badlands had been a farcical substitute.

Later the government decided that the Badlands were unique in their own way, and Badlands National

Park was created. It had the look of terrain from a
science fiction film. Tourists remarked that it certainly was stark, beautiful, *bad* land, and they trav-
eled on to the Black Hills to see the faces of the
presidents. Now Sage leased government land, the
land that had once been part of Pine Ridge but was
now called "public domain," and his stock grazed it.
Even through his darkest days, he had managed to
salvage his claim to the land.

He'd lost the house, but he was replacing it board
by board. He parked the pickup near the barn and
peered between the corral rails. There stood the five
horses for whom the roar of the blue pickup was a call
to dinner. Sage was glad to see them, too. He remembered the day six years ago when he'd sold the last of
his horses. It had been like selling his soul. His uncle
Vern had bought the last two and had given Sage a
terrible look of pity as he'd led them away. Sage never
wanted to see that look again, and he'd vowed to feed
his horses at least as well as he fed himself.

He balanced himself on the top of the corral,
anchoring his boot heels on the second rail. At his
back the five horses ground their oats with teeth that
were as efficient as any millstone. It made good music. In Sage's ears, it was a rich sound. His father had
measured his own success by the number of horses
he'd owned. Sage lifted his head toward the eastern
horizon and watched his cows amble over the hill in
single file, following the well-worn path their prede-
cessors had made for them. He kept them close while
the calves were new, and the stock tank was their wa-

tering hole for now. Later he would move them out to
the hills for better grazing.

Here was more wealth, Sage thought. Fourteen
cows, and all but one had calved successfully. The dry
cow would be sold and replaced. Not many ranchers
would consider fourteen cows a measure of wealth,
but few had learned as Sage had. The cows repre-
sented his effort to rebuild his life. The house was a
symbol, as well. Even in its skeletal state, it was a beginning. It stood on the spot where the old house had
been. Not the one the bank had built when he'd started
out—the one they'd auctioned off and hauled away on
a semi when he'd given up. Not the one the government had built for his parents some twenty years before that—the one they'd called a six-fifty house
because the government had allocated six hundred and
fifty dollars to each tribal member to build the little
three-room structures. No, the new house would stand
where the cabin his family had occupied when he was
a young child once stood.

He was putting it there because he needed to recall
that time. He needed to reconnect himself with those
good memories. The tent the family had lived in during the summer they'd built the log house had stood
near the grove of cottonwoods—only the cottonwoods hadn't been there then. They'd made a base-
ball diamond where the corral now stood, and his
family had been its own team. His father's cousin had
lived with his family, the rival team, four miles away.
Those had indeed been good times, and it was worth
digging back through all the baggage of what his life
had been in the interim to recall them.

He might have pitched a tent for himself for the summer, but he wouldn't finish the house before winter. The little trailer he lived in served his needs adequately. It provided enough hot water for a quick shower, with which he was about to pamper himself, along with a refrigerator large enough to preserve the hamburger he was about to cook and a bed that held all of him but his feet if he slept corner to corner. He worked hard enough during the day so that the size of the bed didn't matter when he finally fell into it at night. Nor did the fact that he slept alone bother him.

He eyed the trailer and thought of Megan McBride. She worked in a little trailer, but he was sure she didn't live in one. In the last few weeks he'd permitted himself one foolish indulgence. From a safe distance he'd watched Megan McBride at work. It hadn't troubled him that a woman was engineering the construction project. In his culture, women took charge as a matter of course, though they spoiled their men in the way of women everywhere. It *had* disturbed him when he realized he'd begun to fantasize about her, but he continued to indulge himself. He watched her assert her authority on the job, and he wondered about the shape of the legs she hid under her jumpsuits. He wondered how strong they were, how agile, how smooth. He knew those heavy work boots must house slender ankles and small, feminine toes.

There were other women in his life—those he met with at least twice a week in the recovery group he'd christened Medicine Wheel. The difference was that Megan McBride was unattainable, which made it safe to think about her. Safe, perhaps, but unwise. He'd come to grips with that fact earlier that day when she'd turned the tables on him. *She'd* watched *him* work. She'd observed his skill, the progress he was making, the way his piece of work fit into the scheme of the project. Those things she'd seen through the eyes of an engineer. But she'd lingered, and he'd felt the scrutiny of a woman's eyes. Later she'd asked him to discuss problems that were human and not mechanical, and another barrier had been ripped away. He saw through her. She was a caretaker, a do-gooder, pure and simple. That was the characteristic that drew them to one another, and the one he had to avoid.

Still, he wondered what she had seen when she'd looked at him through a woman's eyes.

Chapter 2

South Dakota's chain of jewels was the Black Hills. Megan loved her job because it took her outdoors, and this was her favorite part of a state that boasted a wonderful variety of terrain. She had worked her science in all corners of it. Nearly flat farmland stretched over the eastern portion of the state. Heading west, the land began to pucker into rolling hills and buttes that were harbingers of what one would find nearly two hundred miles from the wide Missouri, the river bisecting the state from north to south. But the hint did little to prepare the traveler for that first glimpse of the Hills, which appeared in the distance as a blue-black uprising against a sky that had thoroughly dominated the vista over hundreds of South Dakota miles.

Megan's project involved paving a stretch of gravel running east-west in the southern portion of the Hills. To the east was the Pine Ridge Sioux Indian Reservation. The town of Hot Springs was to the southwest. The tourist's hills, with granite sculptures, gold mines and little towns still rowdy enough to be called Western, stood to the north. Beneath this land lay a maze of caverns, an underground world built by subterranean water and as yet largely unexplored. This tourist's dream could become a highway engineer's nightmare. The initial survey and sample work for this project was proving unreliable.

Karl Taylor straightened slowly as he looked up from the charts that were spread across his "boss lady's" desk. Megan stood on the opposite side, arms folded, waiting for a response. "So how much deeper you think you're gonna go?" he finally asked.

His tone made it clear that he intended to object to her answer, whatever it was. He'd been waiting for a good place to draw the line, and this would be it. Like the South Dakota buttes, his regularly scheduled objections to her decisions had been harbingers of the inevitable uprising.

"I'm projecting ten feet, but it might be more."

"Ten feet! That's a major change in the plans."

"I realize that."

The door opened, and both of them turned as Sage Parker stepped in and closed it behind him. Taylor lifted an accusing eyebrow at Megan as he planted his fist at his waist, which became a hip without the slightest change in contour.

"I sent for Parker because he's running the scraper," Megan said.

"So what? I'm running Parker, along with the rest of the crew."

"*I'm* running the *project*. This stretch has turned out to be a slough." Megan pointed to the map, indicating the area with a closely trimmed fingernail. "We'll dig out the goop even if we have to go down fifteen or twenty feet, and we'll backfill it. I also want to raise the grade so we get better—"

"Raise the grade! You're talking major changes, McBride. Look at this, Parker." Like an anxious woodpecker, Taylor tapped his finger against a spot on the map. "She's talking ten-twenty feet down here, which calls for 'dozing. That scraper by itself won't cut it."

The scene was one Sage would have preferred to walk out on. Taylor was the construction foreman, and McBride was the engineer. It was up to them to have this out, then let him know how to set up his equipment. He would move as much dirt as he was told to move. Against his own better judgment, he stepped closer to the desk and glanced at the fingerprint Taylor had made on the map. He didn't need a picture. He'd been out there digging in it.

"This is a big job, McBride," Taylor said. "And **you're making it bigger. Have you checked with** Krueger?"

"He's out on a site." Megan thrust her hands into the pockets of her jumpsuit. "The changes are necessary," she said quietly. "There's no question."

"There's plenty of question." Taylor gave the map a final tap with his knuckles and turned to Sage. "Wouldn't you say, Parker?"

Sage eyed Taylor's red, round face, then Megan's, which was smooth and tanned that golden shade that only a true blonde seemed to be able to achieve. He figured this threesome could line up two ways: two whites and one Indian, or two men and one woman. For some reason, Taylor had chosen the latter. Tough. Sage glanced down at the map again. "I've paved over this stuff before, Taylor. You have, too. In another year you'll have more potholes than blacktop, and you'll have to resurface."

"So we resurface," Taylor said. "That's not our problem right now. The problem is that the specs don't call for all this digging and backfilling. I say get Krueger out here and see what he says before we make any decisions."

"*We* don't have a decision to make. It's my design," Megan insisted. "It needs to be changed, and I'm changing it."

"Fine." Taylor reached out and snatched the pencil that was perched above Megan's ear. He grinned as he handed it to her. "You go right ahead and change your *design*. Let me know if Krueger approves it." He turned to Sage and nodded toward the door. "Shut the equipment down, Parker. We're knocking off for the day."

Her eyes turned icy, and her jaw became rigid. Sage felt the heat of her humiliation. Out of respect, he did not permit himself to pity her as he told her with a brief look that her self-control had not gone unnoticed. Her glance was just as quick and no less communicative. In good time she would make her point without losing her temper. It was not her knowledge at issue; it was her authority.

Bob Krueger upheld her decision, and the digging proceeded. Krueger warned Taylor against giving Megan any problems, and Taylor cheerfully accepted both the warning and the order to proceed with the changes. Both had come from a man. If they wanted to drag this job out, it was fine with him.

Megan had hoped to see the digging completed before the first inevitable June downpour, but two days later she knew it wasn't to be. Between the subterranean water and the deluge from the sky, the crew was up to its knees in water, and they were again two men short. Taylor's cheer was short-lived.

"I tell you what," Taylor shouted over the roar of a compressor used to power the water pumps. "If those two Indians aren't back on the job tomorrow, I'm gonna ship 'em both off to an equal opportunity cannery."

Megan glanced at Sage, who was busy arranging a compressor hose and had no visible reaction to Taylor's remark. She hoped he hadn't heard it. "Gary called in," she told Taylor. "He couldn't get out to the highway, and he said Jackie's road is pure gumbo."

"Yeah, well, *we're* here." He gestured widely at the men sitting in their cars and pickups. "These guys are here."

The sky was gunmetal gray, and the hilltops were lost in the thickness of it. Megan adjusted the collar of her yellow slicker as another runnel of rainwater slithered down the back of her neck. "This isn't going to break today," she said. "We just need someone to stay and man the pumps."

"Parker!"

Parker, Megan thought. As always, it was Parker. She watched Taylor shout orders into Sage's face. Water dripped from the brim of Sage's orange hard hat as he offered a calm reply. Taylor slogged over to a blue pickup, and Megan heard him tell Randy Whiteman to relieve Sage on the pumps at two o'clock that afternoon.

Heading for his own pickup, Taylor backpedaled a few steps as he announced to Megan, "I'm outta here. If this lets up, I'll see you tomorrow." As he turned on his heel, he slipped, flailed wildly and narrowly missed planting his rump in the mud. "Damn moon dung," he muttered as he took more care trekking across the slick organic goop that was also known to road builders in coarser terms.

Tires spun and threw gravel in their wake as, one by one, the crew members' vehicles took to the road. The unimproved cutoff was closed to through traffic, forcing other drivers to use the longer paved route, which was about a twenty mile jog to the south. On a day like this Megan figured the paved route was certainly preferable, although the plan she was formulating for herself would take her over a long stretch of gravel road within the hour.

The thunk of a closing door drew her head around. Sage had taken shelter in his old blue pickup. She had intended to offer him the office. The gently falling rain tapped on her hard plastic hat. The mud sucked at her work boots as she made her way to the passenger side and rapped at the window. The other door opened, and he did a chin-up over the roof of the cab.

"Come around this side," she was told. "That door doesn't work."

She could hear the seesaw moan of a steel guitar playing on the radio, but he flicked it off when she reached his side. He pushed the door open, and she stuck her head inside. Water dripped from her hat onto his jeans.

"Would you like to use the office?" she asked.

Her face was inches from his, and she was dripping all over him, but he found himself ignoring any inclination to move away. "I need to stay close to the pump in case it clogs up."

"May I speak with you for a moment?"

"Come on in." He slid over.

"I'll get your seat wet."

He laughed and nodded at the puddle she was making under the steering wheel. "You'll get *your* seat wet." He grabbed a faded blue towel from the dashboard and took a swipe at the water. "Give me your slicker. I'll stick it over here with mine."

The wet slickers were piled next to the broken door, and Sage wiped at the seat once more, pulling his hand back just before Megan settled down and pulled the door shut. She dropped her hat to the floor and tossed her head, flinging droplets like a lawn sprinkler. He blotted his face with the towel.

"Oh. I'm sorry."

"Let's face it—" He smiled and tossed her the towel. "We're wet. Should I turn on some heat?"

"Not for me. I'm fine." She gave the hair cropped close to her nape a brisk rub with the terrycloth. "Do you mind doing this?"

"What?"

"Staying to man the pumps."

"It's better than losing a day's pay."

She turned to find that he was watching her. His hair dangled across his forehead and curved over his damp collar like wet, black fringe. The chambray and denim covering his shoulders and his thighs were soaked, and she imagined that his socks were as wet as hers. "I'm glad it's your choice," she said. "Everybody else seems to have specialized, while you're always doing something different. I wondered if Taylor was assigning you whatever nobody else wanted to do."

"Taylor might have a bad mouth on him, but he knows his dirt." Sage raked his fingers through his hair in a vain attempt to push it back from his forehead. "I've got a lot of experience, and he doesn't mind making use of it. Neither do I."

The rain pattered against the roof of the pickup. Megan peered through the windshield at the big yellow bulldozer sitting idle only a few yards away. "Still, nobody likes to sit around all day in wet clothes."

"Then maybe somebody oughta go home and change." He smiled when she turned to him again. "I've been ranching most of my life," he said. "I spend a lot of time in wet clothes."

"And I've got a stop to make before I can go back to Hot Springs, so I'll be wet a while longer, too."

She had yet to give him a hint regarding her purpose for being in his pickup, but he decided it was her prerogative to lead up to whatever it was any way she wanted. She was the boss. "Want some coffee?" he asked. He leaned toward her and reached under her legs, smiling at the wary look she gave him. "It's under the seat."

"Coffee would be great," she said. She tried to stem the shiver that crept along her spine, but it won out, spreading in ripples to her extremities.

Sage tossed the Thermos bottle into his left hand and reached for the keys with his right. "Hit the accelerator," he said as he turned on the ignition. "A little heat wouldn't hurt, either."

"I guess not. I hate it when my socks get wet."

"So do I." He spun the cap on the silver-colored Thermos and stuck it between his knees while he unscrewed the stopper. "Take them off and let them dry out." As he poured, he glanced past the rising steam at the gauges behind the steering wheel. "I've got enough gas to keep the heat on for a while."

"But you have to be able to get home. How far is it?"

"From here to my place? About thirty-five miles." He handed her the coffee he'd poured. "We'll have to share. I don't have an extra cup."

Megan held the cup close to her nose and inhaled the rich aroma of strong, black coffee. The steam warmed her face as she sipped. "Mmm," she murmured between sips. "Perfect."

"I'm gaining a reputation for making good coffee."

"Really? On a day like this you could set up a stand."

He chuckled. "I don't see too many prospective customers."

"Which leads you to wonder why I'm still here." Without meeting his eyes, she handed him the cup.

"Yeah, the thought did cross my mind." He tasted the coffee and decided it wasn't his best. He'd been in a hurry that morning after he'd had to fix a gate the horses had knocked down. But he'd made it to work on time.

She turned toward him and rested her elbow on the steering wheel. "Taylor was gunning for Gary and Jackie again this morning."

"I heard."

"I was afraid you might have." She drew a deep breath and gave a sigh. "I don't want you to take offense at the things he says, Sage."

"Why?"

"Well, because you're doing such a good job. Taylor has such a—"

"No, I mean what's with *you* not wanting *me* to take offense? If I take offense, it'll be between me and Taylor. Why does that concern you?"

"Because Taylor's a bigot, and the project could suffer from his attitude. If he keeps this up and we lose all our Indians—I mean our Native—"

Sage's laughter cut her short. "Lose all our Indians?" He wondered why he was laughing instead of bristling and decided it was either because she looked so pretty sitting there in her wet jumpsuit or because she was trying so damn hard. "Is that anything like losing all our marbles? You're gonna lose yours just trying to figure out what to call us."

"Native Americans." She folded her arms and lifted her chin. "I *meant* to say Native Americans. I know that's what you prefer to be called."

"Who told you that?" He eyed her over the rim of the cup, then sipped the hot coffee.

"I think I read that the preferred term is currently—" She looked at him across the narrow distance between them. There was something steamy about his very presence. She had read that Indians considered it rude to look directly into a person's face, but he was frankly assessing hers. His amusement lingered as a bright sheen in his dark eyes. "I seem to be saying the wrong things again," she said quietly. "What do you prefer to be called?"

"Sage."

He drew a smile from her as he handed her the cup. "It's a very unusual name," she said.

"Lots of Parkers around, but you won't run across too many Sages." He lifted one shoulder. "We've got some Native Americans at Pine Ridge. And we've got some Indians who aren't up on the current term. Columbus called us Indians, but he'd pretty much lost his marbles, too—or his compass, or some damn thing. And America was named for some Italian guy."

"How about Sioux, then?"

"That's the French version of what the Chippewa called us, and it was sort of like being called a snake in the grass. The old ones say we're Lakota, which has nothing to do with being from a certain place or being there first. It means 'allies.'" He raised an eyebrow. "You seem to want to be an ally of the allies."

"I certainly don't want to be an enemy." After swallowing a sip of coffee she added, "I want to be fair."

"And if the Office of Equal Opportunity Employment sends anyone out from Washington, you want them to see minorities working on this project." He laughed. "Hell, they'll see *you*. A woman at the helm oughta be worth at least half a dozen Indians working as flagmen, don't you think?"

"Indians?"

"Or maybe three Native Americans on 'dozers."

"Sage—"

"Or one damn-near civilized Sioux carrying a clipboard and driving a highway department pickup. That could be very impressive."

She passed him the coffee as she held up her other hand in surrender. "Truce, Sage. Please. It isn't just a matter of being in compliance with OEO regulations. I'm really trying to be fair. I know there's very little employment on the reservation, and I'll call you whatever you suggest if you'll just tell me what I can do to persuade Jackie and Gary to stick with us and get to work on time every day."

Sage turned, resting the cup of coffee on his knee, which was bent toward her. He looked at her for a moment, considering the sincerity he saw in her eyes. "What do you want to be called?" She tipped her head to one side, and her eyebrows puckered just slightly. "Like you, I'm kind of at a loss. What do you suggest I call you? Boss lady or Miss McBride?"

"Megan," she said.

"That's simple enough. Okay, Megan, here's the deal. If Taylor tries to make this a racial thing, he'll get trouble. I'll report it. If a guy's not getting to work, you deal with *him*, and you don't generalize the issue to include the rest of us. That's just good supervision."

"I think Taylor has it in for the Indians on the crew."

"You may be right." He offered the cup again. "Want another hit?" She shook her head, so he drained it himself. "*I* think he's got it in for you," he added, gesturing with the empty cup.

"I can handle that."

"And I can handle the other if it comes my way, believe me." The cup clattered against the top of the Thermos as he replaced it, screwing it down tight. "Look, Megan, you've got good instincts, but they're misdirected. Jackie has some growing up to do, and he's determined to do it the hard way. Gary—" He gave a careless shrug. "He'll hold up his end pretty well and cover for himself when he doesn't. You're giving them equal opportunity. You don't have to wipe their noses and pack their lunches for them."

"That isn't what I had in mind. I'm just trying to be—"

"Fair. I know. If the guys from OEO come around, I'll be sure and tell them how you went out of your way to be fair." Not much out of her way, he thought as he studied her face. She didn't have to. With very little makeup her face *was* fair, with smooth, dewy-looking skin and a bow-shaped lower lip that was naturally pink and pouty. He had to keep reminding himself that he was working for her.

"You were dead right about digging this stuff out," he told her. "It's a real deep pocket of pure moon...slime."

She smiled, wondering whether he had chosen his words carefully in deference to her gender or her position. She decided it didn't matter. It was a sign of respect either way. "I *am* good at what I do. And so are you."

"This is what I do to pay the bills," he told her as he slid the Thermos bottle back under the seat. "What I really do is ranch, and I can be good at that, too, when I put my heart into it."

"Are you...do you have a family?"

"Yeah." He sat up slowly, challenging himself to look her straight in the eye and answer this question as easily as he would any other. "I've got two kids. They live with my...They live with their mother in Omaha. We're divorced." There was a womanly softness in her eyes, and he knew he could play on her sympathy if he kept talking about himself. But he'd broken himself of that habit. "What about you? Ever been married?"

She gave her head a quick shake. "No."

"Close?"

"Once. Sort of." Squaring her shoulders, she glanced away. "I've worked hard to get where I am. I haven't had time for much else."

"You know what?" She looked back at him, and he smiled. A fine mist of perspiration gave his face a vigorous luster. "This conversation is getting pretty damn personal. We're fogging up the windows here."

They were surrounded by a silver-gray curtain and vapor-locked together in the cab of his pickup. It gave her a warm, cozy feeling.

"Warm enough yet?"

She looked at him, surprised, wondering whether he'd read her mind. "Oh, yes, and I do need to get going."

He turned off the ignition and pulled the keys. "You never did dry your socks out."

She laughed easily. "I think I can live with wet feet."

"Maybe I can help you out." He unlocked the glove compartment and produced a pair of white tube socks, neatly folded into a military roll. Turning to hand them to her, he caught her puzzled look. He glanced back into the open compartment. She'd seen the small bottle he kept for the more difficult calls he sometimes had to make. "I don't drink on the job, if that's what you're thinking." Closing the compartment, he turned his head and gave her a hard look. It wasn't necessary to tell her anything else, he reminded himself. "I don't drink at all...anymore."

"Why do you have that in there?"

It was none of her business. "For medicinal purposes, believe it or not."

"Cough medicine?"

He didn't laugh. Something in the tone of her voice said she'd heard that excuse before. "It isn't for me."

He reached for her hand. Shock flashed in her eyes when he touched her, and he knew it had to do with the bottle and the fact that she didn't quite believe him. Still, she didn't pull away. He laid the roll of socks in her hand and closed her fingers around them. "I want you to keep your feet warm, Megan. My job may depend on your continued good health."

"What about you?"

"I'll be slogging through this mud until Randy comes on at two o'clock. What good will one pair of socks do me?"

She hardly knew the man. The fact that she was stuffing his socks in her pocket seemed an absolute absurdity. "Thank you."

"Now—" He handed her the top slicker, then picked up his own. "Since I can't see out this window, I'd better go check on the pumps."

"Thank you for the coffee, too." She drew the plastic raincoat around her shoulders, crunching it into the small space between herself and the door. "This conversation has really been helpful."

"Uh-uh, Megan. Watch the sarcasm."

"I mean it," she protested. "You've given me a lot to think about."

He gave her a sidelong glance as he snapped his slicker up the front. The lock of black hair that fell across his forehead made her think of a movie idol striking a sultry pose. "Then let me add one more thought for the day," he said.

"What's that?"

"Projects don't suffer from bigotry. People do." He pushed back the errant lock of hair and settled the bright orange construction worker's hat on his head, offering her a forgiving smile as he explained further. "The Indians aren't yours to lose. And we aren't yours to save, either."

"Did I sound that pompous?" she asked as she retrieved her hat from the floor.

"Yeah. You did." He grinned and jerked his chin toward the door behind her. "After you, Megan. This baby's only got one exit."

Sage shut the compressor off and waded through six inches of water toward a pump that wasn't functioning properly. Water filled his boots and crept up the legs of his jeans. Muttering a curse at the machine, he lifted his head and watched the highway department pickup barrel down the gravel road. He wondered why she was headed east. There was just a little one-horse town between here and Pine Ridge, and surely she didn't have business to do there. As he hauled the pump out of the water he asked himself a more pressing question. Why in the hell had he given that woman his extra pair of socks?

As long as they'd had to shut down for the day, Megan had decided to visit the town of Pine Ridge. In the rain it looked more bedraggled than she'd anticipated. Rows of tract houses, nearly identical except for the assortment of bland pastel colors, stood in various states of disrepair. Funding from the Department of Housing and Urban Development must be harder to come by these days, she thought. In her search for the Bureau of Indian Affairs office build-

ing, Megan passed the Indian Health Service Clinic
and the tribal offices.

Her front tire hit a pothole and splashed a cascade
of water on the words "THORPES NO. 1," which
were spray painted in red on the sidewalk. Megan
knew the high school athletic teams were named for
Jim Thorpe, the versatile Native American Olympic
athlete who'd been stripped of his medals because he'd
earned a few dollars playing semi-professional base-
ball prior to the games. She remembered seeing a film
about him. In later years he'd been plagued by alcoholism.

She had also seen a film about Ira Hayes, the Pima
Indian hero from World War II who'd helped raise the
flag at Iwo Jima. He, too, had struggled with alcoholism. After the war he had been wined and dined by
a country basking in victory and anxious to honor its
heroes. But the country had not been anxious to honor
its debts to the Pima, for whom reservation life meant
poverty and poor health. Megan remembered the
scene in which a drunken Hayes had blacked out and
drowned tragically in two inches of drainage ditch
water.

She needed to assume some of the responsibility for
all this. She wasn't out to save anyone, but there had
been so much unfairness in the past. In her position,
she needed to go out of her way to be fair. Sage was
right. She was certainly naive in these matters, and she
wanted to learn.

She'd taken some engineering classes from Pete Petersen, who was in charge of the BIA Roads Department at Pine Ridge. He recognized her immediately

when she walked into his office, and he offered her more coffee and all the time she wanted.

"I hear you've got Sage Parker on your project," Pete said after the initial amenities and personal news had been exchanged. "He's spent a few seasons working for me. Good man. Damn good man, long as he stays sober. He's not one of the ones you're concerned about, is he?"

Megan flexed her foot and glanced past her crossed knees at the toe of her work boot as she paused to appreciate the fact that she was wearing dry socks. "Not at all," she reported. "I don't think there's a piece of equipment on the site he can't handle, and he's there every day, just like clockwork."

"He was a heavy equipment operator when he was in the Army years back. Kind of a local hero in his day, too. Hell of a bull rider. Had a pretty little wife. 'Course, everybody around here wants to ranch, and he did that, too. Sage had it all." The springs in Pete's desk chair squeaked as he leaned back and folded his hands over his droopy paunch. "Guess every one of us has at least one lesson to learn the hard way."

"What happened?" Megan asked.

"Sage always was a hard worker. Used to be a hard drinker and a hard swinger, too." Pete shook his head slowly as he tapped his thumbs together. "When the bubble burst, Sage came down harder than most. He had a lot to lose, and he lost it all. First time he went up to Fort Meade for treatment for alcoholism, they had to drag him kicking and screaming. They say he checked himself into a different program the second time around."

"I understand he's running a recovery program of his own now."

"Kind of a post-treatment program, I guess. They talk about traditional values and reviving the community. He calls it the Medicine Wheel." Pete sat up quickly. The springy chair swatted him in the back as he planted his elbows on the desk. "Yep," he drawled. "Some people around here think ol' Sage walks on water. Others want to see his program slide right down the tubes."

"Why?"

His humorless smile gave his answer a chilling edge. "Business. You got your liquor sales, your pawn brokers, your loan sharking. Those people are making money."

"Off other people's misery," Megan reflected.

"That's right. That's the way of the world, I'm afraid. One man gets well, and he goes out tilting at windmills. The blood-suckers start gunning for him." Pete slapped his palm against the desktop and smiled. "Damn, I hope he knocks a few of them flat on their butts. They've got a hearing going on in the tribal office at four o'clock." He checked his watch. "If they're running on Indian time, it should be getting started about now. It's four-thirty. Sage and some of the others want to see the council deny liquor license renewals on the reservation. You oughta take a walk over there—give a listen. Might be an eye-opener for you, Megan."

Chapter 3

Pete Petersen accompanied Megan to the tribal office building, where the meeting was in progress. They shook the water from their raincoats and made their way toward the double doors. Pete shouldered a path through the lingerers, and Megan followed closely behind him.

A man standing near the door directed them to two folding chairs. Megan noticed that people preferred to stand against the walls and gather near the door rather than fill the seats that had been provided for spectators. She was happy to take a seat, where she could keep a low profile. She'd felt people's curiosity as scores of dark eyes followed her from the door to the chair. Glancing around her at the sea of brown faces, Megan realized that this was the first time she'd been the racial minority in a crowd of people. She pushed her damp hair back behind her ears and slouched self-consciously, wondering whether her presence was viewed as an intrusion.

Her interest soon supplanted her discomfort. Pete tipped his balding head toward her and pointed out the tribal chairman, who sat on the dais with two other officers, and the councilmen, whose tables formed two sides of a square flanking the dais. The witness' table and the rows of spectators' chairs behind it completed the square. A young woman was speaking into the witness' microphone, and a child continually reached for her from the lap of a man who sat close by. Megan leaned sideways for a better view and discovered that the man was Sage Parker.

He shifted the toddler from one knee to the other and bounced him occasionally. The youngster attempted a quick slide over Sage's thigh, but a protective arm brought him up short and settled him back in place. Megan caught a glimpse of the little boy's black-eyed scowl as Sage pulled the small blue and white striped T-shirt down over his round little belly. Sage, too, appeared to listen with one ear, and he handled the baby as naturally as he did a jackhammer.

Megan leaned in Pete's direction and whispered, "Who's the speaker?"

"That's Jackie Flying Elk's wife, Regina. She's a beauty, isn't she?"

For some reason, she hadn't imagined Jackie with a beautiful wife. With the number of heads in her way, Megan couldn't see much besides the woman's long, satiny fall of black hair, and that was enough to trigger a pang of envy. Megan kept her own hair short. It was comfortable, practical, easy to care for and perfectly suited to her line of work. Secretly, though, she coveted long hair, and Regina's was worth coveting. The child on Sage's lap thought so, too, and he nearly managed to snatch a handful of it before Sage caught him. He brought the little hand to his mouth and playfully nipped the child's fat fingers. It was a side of the man Megan had not imagined, and it gave her a warm feeling just to watch. Mingled with the warmth was something else—something strangely akin to that envy of a woman who had something Megan might want.

"Is that her child?" Megan whispered.

"Which one?" Pete craned his neck for a glimpse past a dozen rows of intervening heads. He smiled. "Oh, yeah, there's Sage. Figured he'd be here." Then, in answer to the question, he shrugged. "Probably Regina's. Sage's kids are older. Besides, the wife took them somewhere out of state. From what I hear, she won't let him near them."

The boy on Sage's lap wasn't the only young child in the room. The voices of several others, along with the continual shuffle of people moving in and out of the room, caused an undercurrent that seemed to disturb no one but Megan. She was annoyed with herself when she realized that Regina had concluded her remarks, and Megan had heard little of what she'd said. She listened to Regina's response to a question from one of the councilmen. Yes, Regina was aware that revoking the license in question would not force the closing of all the bars on the reservation, but she hoped it would be a start.

"That's the guy they're trying to close down." Pete's nod directed Megan's attention to a brawny white man who was sitting near the exit at the front of the room. His ruddy complexion contrasted strikingly with hair and eyebrows the color of wheat. "Floyd Taylor owns one of two bars and the only grocery store in Red Calf, a little town about thirty miles north of here. If you didn't blink as you passed, you might have noticed it off to the east."

"I saw the sign," Megan whispered. "He's not related to Karl Taylor, is he?"

"Floyd's his younger brother. They've got three more built just like them."

If Floyd's personality was anything like Karl's, Megan already knew where her sympathies lay in this issue. She'd never joined the crew at the Red Rooster, their favorite happy hour spot, because she had no interest in finding out what kind of conversation Karl Taylor might make after a few beers.

Floyd Taylor raised his hand like a schoolboy as he came to his feet. "Mr. Chairman? I'd like to ask Mrs. Flying Elk a question, if I could." No one objected as the big blond barkeeper turned toward the witness table. "I'd just like to know if I'm to blame for the way your husband drinks, Mrs. Flying Elk. Are you saying it's my fault he ended up back in detox again?"

Regina's voice was strong and clear. "No, Mr. Taylor. I'm not saying it's your fault."

"It just seems to me that's what this is all about, this hearing. I'm a businessman. I abide by the laws, both tribal and state, and I do business with whoever comes in the door, unless he's under age." Taylor waved a hand about the room. "I see a lot of familiar faces in this room, and, hell, you all know me. Old Uncle Floyd. You come to me when you need gas money, when you've got a sick kid, or when you just run a little short at the end of the month, and I don't turn you down." His open-handed gesture was directed at Regina. "Everybody's welcome at Floyd's, but I never twisted anybody's arm, Mrs. Flying Elk. Your husband's a big boy, and he makes his own decisions."

"I know that," Regina said. "My husband is not the issue."

"Then what is?"

"Didn't you hear one word of what I said, Mr. Taylor?"

"Mrs. Flying Elk," the chairman said through his microphone, "is there anything you want to add to your statement at this time?"

"I've said all I have to say." She pushed her chair back and leaned forward to add, "Anyone who has no ears won't hear me anyway. Thank you, Mr. Chairman."

Regina moved to the chair next to Sage's and took the child from his lap. Two more speakers took the chair behind the witness table and offered prepared statements, but impromptu testimony from the floor was permitted, as well. Characteristic of each speech were the final words, "That's all I have to say." Much of the testimony gave personal witness to the far-reaching effects of alcohol within the community and ended with a plea for the people, as a whole, to reject its use. Megan heard the courage in each speaker's voice as heart-rending stories were offered publicly, but she knew that none of this would convict Floyd Taylor of anything in a court of law.

On the other side, people claimed that they should all have the right to choose for themselves. "If they're gonna drink, they're gonna drink," one man said. "We've got enough bootleggers around here now, selling to minors. It'll be worse if we close the bars down."

Finally, Sage came to the microphone. The room grew quieter, and there was a sense of expectation as he arranged several manila folders on the table. Megan wondered how he'd managed to work until two, stop to change into his red Western shirt and a pair of jeans that were certainly newer and drier than the ones he'd been wearing earlier, and get here for this meeting. He'd obviously defied all speed limits.

His introductory remarks reviewed his reasons for filing with the tribal court for an injunction against the renewal of Floyd Taylor's liquor license. From a file of police reports he cited numerous complaints against Taylor for disturbing the peace, serving liquor to customers who were clearly intoxicated and serving minors. In some cases Taylor had paid a nominal fine. In others no one would testify against him, or the testimony of a few had been refuted by a greater number, and the issue had died quietly.

"Mr. Taylor is not responsible for one man's relapse," Sage argued, "but he is responsible to this community to uphold its laws. Even when he gets off on a technicality, we all know what he's doing. We all know that 'Uncle Floyd' doesn't give a damn about our sick kids, or about the kids that this complaint alleges were sitting out in the car in front of the bar until two o'clock in the morning—'' he waved a paper in Taylor's direction ''—keeping nearby residents awake with their crying.''

"Those kids aren't my responsibility," Taylor injected.

"When you continue to serve their parents long after neither one can stand up, whose responsibility are they, Taylor? Why didn't you call the police?"

"What difference does it make?" Floyd slouched back in his chair and waved the matter away with one hand. "Somebody called the police, and the whole thing was taken care of without any trouble. You know I don't let kids in at Floyd's."

"Not unless they've got the price of a drink," Sage grumbled.

"Hey, look, I do my best. I can't always be sure how old they are." A slow grin crossed Floyd's face. "You know damn well you got by a time or two, Sage. 'Course, that was when my dad was running the place, and the law wasn't as tough then. Speaking of which . . ." The smug-faced man braced his hands on his knees and leaned forward. "I can think of a few times when it was *your* kids out in the car."

There was a moment of heavy silence before Sage's voice came over the microphone again. "I'm paying the price for that, Taylor. My children are no longer living with me."

Megan felt a tightness in her chest as she drew her next breath. A shared sense of despair pervaded the room. Those with children drew them closer, and most of the others hung their heads.

"Mr. Chairman." Attention turned to the council-man who had broken the silence. "I move we table this matter. We need time to look over the reports Mr. Parker has gathered."

The motion was passed, and the meeting was quickly adjourned. Sage put the papers back in their folders and took them to the chairman. As he walked back from the dais, he saw Megan. He hesitated as though he'd lost his bearings for a moment. She smiled and waited near her chair, thinking he would come over and speak to her. Instead he acknowledged her with a nod, then turned his attention to the people who had been sitting near him.

Ignoring a quick surge of disappointment, she took her raincoat from the back of the chair and offered Pete a handshake. "Thanks for your time, Pete. This was interesting. How long do you think the debate will continue?"

"I don't know. Taylor wants it settled. That injunction keeps him from doing business."

"It sounds as though he shouldn't *be* in business," she said as she and Pete moved with the crowd toward the door.

"There are a lot of sides to this issue. Some people would accuse Sage's group of angling toward a return to Prohibition."

"I didn't get that impression." When they reached the lobby, Megan put on her raincoat. "I hope this lets up soon," she said, nodding toward the rain streaming down outside the doors. "I'm battling ground water as well as rain."

"Project's getting interesting, huh?" Pete pulled a floppy canvas hat down over his brow. "You were the first woman ever enrolled in any of my classes. Not that I've done that much teaching, but you did come as a surprise." He offered a warm smile, full of a teacher's pride in a student-made-good. "You'll do fine."

Megan dashed down the sidewalk and hopped across the rivulet of water that washed past the curb. Within the shelter of her pickup, she shucked her raincoat and stuffed it under the front seat. She was combing her fingers through her damp hair when the door on the passenger side swung open and Sage slid into the seat. Water dripped from the brim of his straw cowboy hat, and the shoulders of his denim jacket were wet. He tossed the hat on the seat between them and angled his body toward her.

"You drove a long way to satisfy your curiosity."

The guarded look in his eyes was unsettling. She found herself searching for excuses. "Pete Petersen was a teacher of mine. I came to ask for some advice. I didn't know about the hearing, but when he suggested . . . I thought I could learn more about . . ."

"And did you?"

"Yes, I did. I learned a great deal."

He seemed to stare right through her, and she imagined that her forehead had become a message display board betraying her every reaction to what she had just observed. She fussed with her hair again and wished he would stop looking at her that way. Finally he turned his attention to the dollops of rainwater that splashed on the windshield from an overhanging cottonwood tree.

"Even if we lose this one in the end, it's worth the effort," he said. Megan wondered whether he was confiding in her or simply coming to terms with something he'd decided was likely to occur. "It's a chance to bring things out in the open and make people take a look."

"With all those complaints, it's really shocking that they haven't closed Floyd Taylor down before this."

"Shocking?" He watched a small, waferlike cottonwood seed slide down the glass. "Was that the only thing you heard in there that shocked you?"

"I wasn't really shocked," she confessed quietly. "I don't live in a vacuum. I don't want to, anyway. That's why I came."

"To take a firsthand look at how the other half lives?"

"To *learn*, Sage. It's important to be sensitive to the fact that an employee is a human being and to deal with him as a person rather than a machine." She knew she sounded like something out of a book, but she couldn't seem to stop herself. "In order to do that, I have to—"

"Sensitive." He smiled at the windshield. "I like that." After a moment he turned his head, and his eyes became mellow as he looked at her. "Do you realize how soft that makes you sound?"

"A man like Karl Taylor might mistake sensitivity for weakness." Her eyes narrowed. "I didn't think you would."

"I didn't say weak. I said soft." He propped his elbow on the back of the seat and rested his temple against his prominent knuckles. "A lot of people are willing to drive extra miles to avoid passing through a reservation. They're sure we lie in wait to slash their tires and siphon their gas." He raised one dark eyebrow. "Since you're here, I guess I can't call you weak."

"I'm not soft, either." She folded her arms to cover her breasts.

There was little cheer in the smile he gave her. "And these aren't your tires. So what do you think all this sensitivity leads to?"

"Fairness," she said.

"Oh, yeah." He snapped his fingers. "I remember now. You're the one who's determined to be fair."

"I want to deal fairly with everyone, and I don't think that necessarily means dealing with all people in exactly the same way. I'm here to learn more about—"

"You being the dealer makes it pretty nice. You get to deal out second chances whenever you're feeling particularly sensitive." He eyed her with a challenge. "Do I get one?"

"I don't know," she answered quietly. She'd seen him expose himself before the crowd. He hadn't asked for sympathy then. What was he asking for now? "I think you're asking the wrong person."

She'd struck the right chord. He closed his eyes and used his fingertips to smooth the creases from his brow. "Sometimes I think I owe the whole world an apology, and I don't like the feeling." He lowered his

hand and offered a tentative smile, made genuine this
time by the soft luster in his eyes. "I was just taking a
guilt trip and looking for a traveling companion."

"I'm sorry about your children, Sage."

"Uh-uh." He jabbed his chest with his thumb. "I'm
the one who's sorry. What Taylor said about my ne-
glect—that part was true." His sigh was a long, hollow sound. He settled back against the seat and
watched two drenched figures hurry past the hood of
the pickup. "I can go to these meetings and say all the
things that need to be said, and they can say, 'Who the
hell do you think you are? We all know you.' And they
tell me who I am. They remind me. Every damn time."

"Two people so far have told me who you are,"
Megan said. Her heart had ballooned with sympathy
at the sound of his sigh, but she was determined to
deflate the feeling to a size and shape that might be
more acceptable to him. "Bob Krueger and Pete Petersen both said you were the best man on my crew.
They said—"

"They said I'm a hell of a good worker when I'm
sober, and they'd heard I've really straightened out."

"They *knew* you've straightened out. It's been several years, hasn't it?"

"Four. I've got an anniversary coming up." He
chuckled. "I never remembered my wedding anniversary, but I remember the day I quit drinking. I remember the hour."

"I understand you've started a recovery group," she
said. "Is it like Alcoholics Anonymous?"

"Yeah, pretty much." He realized that he'd already entrusted her with a great deal more about him-

self than he'd intended, but Medicine Wheel was something beyond himself. He offered his customarily vague explanation. "It's a group effort."

"Nobody approved of the tactics Taylor used," Megan assured him.

Sage lifted one shoulder in a shrug. "The man's fighting for his livelihood. He'll use all the ammunition that's available to him, and I spent a lot of years building that munitions dump." He turned to her again and saw the look of expectation in her eyes. He was confiding in her, and she liked that. She was an outside pair of ears, and he wanted to talk. "Some of these people remember Prohibition, and they think we're trying to bring it back."

"That was a long time ago."

"Not for us," he said. "It wasn't until the 1950s that the laws began to permit the selling of liquor to reservation Indians. The people went to bootleggers instead of bars. Then they sat in their cars or went out behind the privy and slugged it down. That's the way we drink—like we're afraid a hand's going to reach out of the dark and take it away from us. We haven't cultivated any social drinking skills."

"You're certainly not alone in that."

"Maybe not, but I sure wish the old whiskey drummers and the bootleggers had brought along those classy traditions. You know, the etiquette—the towel over the arm and checking out the cork." He smiled, and his brown eyes brightened. "Aren't you impressed by a guy who knows how to order wine?"

"I haven't given it much thought."

"I have. Just lately, since I started trying to put the pieces together. I want to know, 'Why us?'" He braced his hand against the dashboard. "We have beautiful, old traditions, but not one of them has anything to do with having a drink before dinner. Hell, Muscatel comes with a screw cap, and who can tell anything about its 'bouquet' when you're passing the bottle with a bunch of guys behind the outhouse?"

Her laughter sputtered in her throat, and it was useless to try to hold it in. This wasn't something she wanted to laugh about, but the image he'd conjured up was wonderfully absurd. The heavy weight of her sympathy was lifted by the fact that they laughed together.

"Does Muscatel have a bouquet?" she managed.

"They used to call it 'Mustn't Tell.' I suppose 'Mustn't Smell' fits, too."

"Oh, Sage." Her laughter wound down, and she shook her head. "This isn't something we should laugh about."

"Why shouldn't we? Don't you know how much Indian people like to laugh? Through it all, we have to be able to laugh."

The notion seemed strange to her. Serious matters were to be met with complete gravity, and, she had to admit, she didn't know how much Indian people liked to laugh. "What's the difference between Prohibition and what you're trying to do?"

He ticked the points off without a moment's hesitation, because he knew them well. "I don't want *them* to tell *us* we can't drink. I want *us* to decide we won't. I want us to say *no*, individually and collectively. I want Taylor and his kind to be out of business simply because we don't want what he's got to sell. Every one of us suffers from it."

"Obviously not everyone agrees."

"Not yet, but we're growing in number." His conviction brightened his dark eyes. "Even if we lose, we've got people talking about it. Traditionally our decisions were made by consensus, which is hard to get. You have to keep talking, keep reminding people."

"Your meetings seem to offer everyone a chance to say his piece."

"That's right," he said with a quick nod. He lifted one finger to punctuate his promise. "You get a circle of Indian people together, and you'll hear some speeches. We love to make speeches, and we have a style all our own."

"Was it an intrusion?" she asked, suddenly worried. "My being there today, I mean."

"No, it wasn't. I guess I got a little defensive." His eyes were bright, and his smile spread slowly. The damp hair that fell across his forehead gave him an unexpectedly boyish look. "I wasn't expecting the 'boss lady' to be part of the audience."

"And I didn't come to spy on you." She returned his smile. "I wouldn't do that to someone who loaned me dry socks."

Sage knew he had to be crazy. For the second time in one day he was sitting in a pickup with this too-cute lady from Pierre while a curtain of rain dropped around them, interfering with his fragile connection with reality. And he was grinning about it.

* * *

Two weeks later Megan recalled every word that had passed between them in that pickup as she considered her problem with Karl Taylor. Sage hadn't said that she *was* soft. He'd said that the importance she placed on sensitivity made her *sound* soft. She hadn't been offended, because he hadn't been offensive. Taylor *had*—once too often. Bob Krueger had agreed to take him off the project.

Megan slid her report into a manila envelope and sealed it carefully. Her complaint would become part of Taylor's personnel file, and he would be reprimanded. Off the record, there would be those who would reiterate the notion that this was a man's job, and any woman who demanded the right to be out here with a road crew might expect an occasional sexual hassle. That notion had become obsolete, Megan reminded herself as she peered through her office window in time to watch Bob Krueger pull up in a highway department car. Bob wasn't there to give Taylor the news. Megan had done that herself, and since he hadn't shown up for work that morning, she assumed he'd gone to the State Highway Department office in Pierre. Bob was there to pick up her written complaint and to discuss replacing Taylor.

Bob listened to her tell her story exactly as she had told it over the phone. She needed to repeat it, and he saw her frustration in the way she waved her arms about, heard it in the way her voice kept climbing as she spoke. She wouldn't be bullied or manhandled, but she was still trying to convince herself that she'd been absolutely fair.

"So there were no witnesses," he concluded as he leaned across her desk and stubbed his cigarette out in the jar lid she'd put there for him.

Megan stood beside the window and watched an earth mover crawl up a hill. "There was no one else around," she confirmed.

"And this was the first time Taylor tried anything like this?"

Megan sighed. "It was the first clearly overt gesture. A couple of times he made a point to cut off my space—make me walk around him. He made a stupid remark once, and I told him he was way out of line."

"But this time he actually cornered you."

She nodded toward the metal cabinets and patiently repeated, "Against the files."

"And told you . . ."

"That my skin looked so soft it made his palms itch. It's in the report, word for word."

"And you told him . . ."

"To get the hell out of my way."

"Which he did." Bob leaned back in his chair. "I'm not defending these guys, Megan, but this kind of thing has happened before. By my count this is the third time."

She folded her arms tightly as she turned from the window. "It may not be the last. It's not a man's world anymore, Bob. I don't come equipped with a black belt in karate. I don't have to. I know the law."

"Taylor does, too. I knew you weren't a good match, but I wanted his experience." Bob dismissed his mistake with a wave of the hand. It was time to move on. "We've got so damn many projects going this summer. I've got everybody working. You said you've got a replacement in mind?''

Megan nodded. "Parker."

"That's what I thought. He's the logical choice." Bob shook his head slowly. "He won't do it, Megan. I've offered it to him before."

"*This* job?"

"Not this project, but others." With a smile, Bob remembered, "He doesn't want to give orders, he says. He just wants to work."

Megan turned toward the window again. Sage was the right man for the job, she told herself. The fact that she liked him wasn't a crime. The crew liked him, too. He was *likable*, for heaven's sake. He was also capable, which was why she had chosen him. "I'm going to offer him the position anyway," she said firmly. "With his experience and his skills, *he* knows he's the logical choice. It would be unfair not to offer it to him."

When Sage saw the dark green car parked next to the office, he knew his lunch break was shot. Megan had sent for him, Krueger was there, and he'd heard about Taylor. It wasn't hard to put one and one and one together and foresee the "great opportunity" on the horizon. As he mounted the wobbly metal steps to the trailer, he slapped some of the dust off the seat of his jeans and buttoned a couple of shirt buttons, leaving two still open. Hell, it was too hot to dress for the occasion.

"You wanted to see me?" Sage glanced from the man seated near the desk to the woman standing behind it. He wasn't sure whose idea this was, but he figured he could handle both of them if it became a joint effort.

"We've had to pull Taylor off this project," Bob announced. "You probably heard."

"Sure, I heard." He'd been hearing it all morning from the guys who'd been with Taylor at the Red Rooster the night before. And all morning long he'd resisted the temptation to storm the office and demand to know what that jerk had said to her, what he'd *really* done. Sage had had to remind himself that he wasn't her champion; he was part of her construction crew. She'd obviously taken care of the situation quite efficiently. It was none of Sage's business what Taylor had said or done, but when he looked at Megan this time, he knew damn well that his eyes conveyed his concern.

"I want you to take over as construction supervisor," she said simply.

"I don't want the job."

The offer obviously came as no surprise to him. Megan moved to the front of the desk and stood as rigidly as he did. "You should have had it to begin with. With all your skills, it's time you moved ahead in this business."

"Who says I want to move ahead?" He spoke to her as though explaining a new concept. "I need a job, Miss McBride. I need to put food on my table, gas in my bulk tank, and pay my child support. I don't need a foreman's headaches."

"Some foremen *cause* headaches," Megan pointed out. "Properly handled, this job—"

"Sage." Bob came to his feet slowly. "I know you've turned us down before. I also know you're trying to rebuild that ranch of yours." He adjusted his pants, rested his hands at his hips and smiled. "You'll damn near double your pay with this job, son. *Double* it. You'll be that much closer to getting that place back on its feet."

Sage had anticipated this argument, too. It was the one point the idea had in its favor. He'd never gotten along very well with money, but it was hard to get along without it. And it was impossible to build much of a cattle operation without it. He turned away and shoved his hands in his back pockets. "A foreman doesn't make an engineer's decisions," he reflected. "And an engineer lets the foreman handle the crew." He turned and gave Megan a pointed look. "You don't seem to want to work it that way, though."

"Taylor was letting his racial and sexual prejudices influence his decisions. Nothing works very well *that* way."

"What makes you think it'll work my way? You and I might be worse news yet."

Megan smiled as she held out the ring of keys Taylor had relinquished when he left the site. "I think it's worth a try."

Chapter 4

They'd stopped asking him to join them at the Rooster after work, but Sage always knew which of the crew had been there when he saw them the next morning. With Scott it meant sunglasses, and Randy drank a lot of coffee, no matter how hot the weather was. Gary wasn't talking to anyone this morning. And Jackie wasn't there.

Sage squinted into the sun as he approached the trio. Randy drained his Thermos cup while Gary leaned on a shovel handle and scowled at the approach of authority. "You guys taking another break?" Sage asked.

"It's hot," Scott grumbled. "We're thirsty."

Sage nodded. "Rough night, huh?" Gary propped his foot on the shoulder of the shovel blade. "You can either give me the time back at noon or after five,"

Sage said quietly. "You guys haven't done a damn thing all morning."

"This job's going to your head, Sage." Randy's affable smile enabled him to say almost anything without causing offense. "You know, Taylor had a mean mouth on him, but, times like this, he'd usually cut us some slack."

"You're not working for Taylor anymore." Sage looked at Gary, who appeared to be ignoring the conversation. "Did you see Jackie last night?" Gary lifted his shoulder and wiped his face against his sleeve, but he gave no answer. Sage glanced back at Randy, then at Scott. "Listen, I don't give a damn what you guys do on your own time, but when you come to work, you be ready to put in an eight-hour day."

Sage watched the three men in his rear-view mirror as he pulled away slowly in his pickup. They'd gone grudgingly back to the chore of laying gravel and clay as a base for the blacktop that was to come. Gary was mad because he'd been taken off the gravel truck. Randy was mad because Sage hadn't smiled back and told him everything was okay, and Scott was mad because his head hurt. Sage knew how that went, and, at the moment, he didn't much like his three-week-old job. A cloud of dust veiled the reflections in the mirror as Sage pressed the accelerator to the floor.

One truth he'd discovered about himself was that he didn't much like being disliked. In his drinking days he'd been in his glory when people were cheering for him, or slapping him on the back and calling him "friend." In his drinking days he would have told those three to take it easy today, and he would have relished the acceptance he would have gotten in return. He told himself that he didn't need that anymore. That was yesterday. Today he had a job to do, and if he did it well, he could get some satisfaction out of it. He didn't have to please the crew, and they didn't have to like him. They had to respect him. So he had to give them something worth respecting.

Jackie's car was parked near the office. Sage muttered a curse as he gripped his own steering wheel and arced it to park the pickup alongside the car. Jackie was asleep with his mouth open and his neck arched over the top of the seat. When Sage tapped on the roof to wake him, Jackie jerked his head up and looked around.

"Hey, Sage." He squeezed one eye shut and squinted through the other. "Sorry I'm late. Thought I'd check the office first, then follow your tracks."

Sage squatted next to the car door to put his eyes on a level with Jackie's. "You been home yet?" *Don't lie to me, Jackie,* he pleaded silently.

"Sure." Jackie grinned. "Sure, I been home. I'm okay, Sage. The alarm clock didn't work is all."

Jackie's breath smelled like sewer water. "Guess you forgot to brush your teeth, huh?" *It's too late, Jackie. Spare yourself the indignity of lying to me.*

"Yeah. I was in a hurry." The smile faded, and Jackie played his trump—the one reference that might gain him sympathy. "The ol' lady'll throw me out if I lose this job. She's countin' on fixing an old house up into a store. Smart woman." He grinned again. "So whatcha got for me today? Gravel or oil?"

"Your last paycheck. I'm sorry, Jackie." Sage straightened slowly and patted the roof of the car a couple of times the way he would the man's shoulder if it had been handier. "Go on back to sleep. I don't want you on the road again till you've slept it off." He turned and headed for the office, where he saw movement in the window.

"Hey, Sage, I'm okay. I swear it!"

Sage stopped and turned back toward the car. "Let me know when you're ready for treatment, Jackie. I'll drive you to Fort Meade myself."

Megan was waiting for him. He avoided her eyes as he reached for the clipboard on his desk.

"Are you sure he's been drinking?"

He looked up. His eyes hardened when he saw that innocent expression. She wanted him to be prosecutor, judge and jury while she played the bleeding-heart advocate. "Did you talk to him?"

"Yes, I did. He came to the office first."

He turned to the list on his clipboard and added some figures. She wasn't stupid. She was as sure as he was.

"You fired him."

Was that an accusation or an observation? "I read the policy. I intend to follow it."

"I think if you gave him something—the promise of a job, maybe—he might opt for treatment. There's a provision for that in the policy, you know."

The clipboard clattered when he tossed it on the desk. "I know about the provision." His eyes glittered with resentment, not at her, but at what he'd had to do. "Jackie knows about it, too, and he knows how to ask. He's been there before."

"Maybe he can't ask."

"Then maybe he's not ready."

"He needs help, Sage."

They heard the roar of an engine, and they both turned toward the window. Sage took two steps closer in time to watch Jackie pull away in a hail of gravel. "Damn. I told him to wait."

"For what?" Megan asked.

"I told him to go back to sleep for a while."

She folded her arms and injected a note of sarcasm into her voice. "You fired him, and then you expected him to curl up and go to sleep on our doorstep?"

"*Our* doorstep?" He whirled from the window and jabbed a finger into the air. "This is *your* doorstep. Mine's thirty-five miles east of here." And if Jackie showed up on *his* doorstep, Sage would give him his bed and make his own in the cab of his pickup. But he wouldn't tell Megan that.

She pointed toward the window. "You can't fire a man and not expect him to go off hurt and angry like that."

"How many men have you fired?" He shouted the question and allowed two seconds for an answer. Her blue eyes flashed her message of defiance. "That's what I thought. Look, if you're out to save drunks, you oughta get yourself into another line of work." He jerked his head in the direction she'd indicated. "Go after him. Go on! Coax him. Persuade him to get treatment again."

"What would be wrong with that?" She clenched her fists in the shelter of her armpits and loosed the stinging dart. "How many times have *you* needed treatment, Mr. Parker?"

His voice was steely and cold. "None of your damn business."

She wanted to bite her tongue. "You're right. That wasn't—"

"First you hired me to blast rock and dig out a road, and all I had to worry about was moving dirt. Now you've got me moving people. I don't enjoy moving people, Miss McBride." Anger dissolved as the realization dawned in his brain. "But I can do it. And since the job's mine, I *will* do it."

He moved toward the door and turned with one quiet comment. "You can't save drunks, Megan. It can't be done that way. But you come to a Medicine Wheel meeting sometime, and you can watch how they save themselves."

He climbed into his truck and headed downhill from the office toward the site where more earth work had been started. Halfway down the hill, the pickup lunged toward the shoulder, and Sage fought with the shuddering steering wheel with one hand while he downshifted with the other. The pickup lurched, listed to the right, and stopped. Sage glanced at the hood ornament and the empty air beyond, where the gravel gave way to a fifty-foot drop-off. His left hand was cramped from the strain of holding the wheel, and his right trembled. He pushed the door open and stumbled out.

"What happened?"

Sage looked up as he stepped back from the pickup. Megan was running toward him, and the words "to the rescue" flitted across his mind as he turned back to survey the crippled vehicle. "What happened?" he muttered as he hitched his hands on his hips. "The damn wheel fell off, obviously."

"I know," she panted. With a wave of her hand, she told him, "It's back there. I mean, what *happened*? How did it just—"

"How the hell do I know?" He stalked off, climbing the gravel hill well ahead of her. He hoped she hadn't noticed the way he was shaking. Maybe it didn't show on the outside.

"Good Lord, you almost went off the—"

"I know!"

The hubcap lay twenty feet from the tire, but he didn't see any lug nuts anywhere. A piece of paper was stuffed into the rim, and the rim itself wasn't even bent. The whole damn thing had just flown off! Not without help, he decided as he jammed the paper into his pocket before Megan reached him with her next question.

"What was that?"

He came to his feet and glanced away as she stepped up to him. "Nothing. Just a piece of . . . trash."

"Trash?"

"Trash. Road trash." Mentally he measured the distance he'd driven before the tire fell off as he viewed the top of the hill. It wasn't much. "You wanna help me find those lug nuts?"

"Lug nuts?"

"Is there something wrong with the way I pronounce these words? Trash," he said with exaggerated care. "And lug nuts." He started up the hill.

"I don't understand why you're picking up trash at a time like this." She scowled as she followed, scouring the road.

"Seems as good a time as any. Litter just brings tears to my eyes."

She ignored the sarcasm. "Sage, I think someone might have tampered with your pickup."

"Really." He knelt to retrieve one of the nuts he was looking for.

"You don't think it could have been...Jackie?" She angled to the left. "Here's another one."

"He didn't have time."

"Did you see anyone else around?"

"I was too busy arguing with you. How many have you got?"

"Two."

"One more."

"You know, you're entitled to the use of a department vehicle now."

"I'd rather drive my own." He spied another glint of silver in the dirt and picked up his pace.

"Why?"

"It's got character." And it didn't have South Dakota Highway Department emblazoned on the side. Randy's suggestion that the job had gone to his head had hit a nerve. He didn't want to wear any badges. He didn't even like having a desk. All he'd need was a sign on his pickup and they'd all hate him.

"You don't think it was someone who resented your getting this job, do you?"

"Hell, I don't know!" He rose from the ground with the last of the lug nuts. He looked up, saw her standing there, saw the concern in her eyes and felt like a piece of road trash himself. "Look, I'm sorry." With a nod of his chin he indicated the pickup. From the higher vantage point they could see just how close he'd come to careening over the edge. "That scared the hell out of me," he confessed.

"Me, too."

He gave a nervous laugh. Her, too? Why not? he asked himself. Who'd want to see somebody drive his pickup off a cliff? It didn't have to mean anything *personal*.

She lifted her arm slowly and opened her hand. His fingertips dragged lightly over the center of her palm as he claimed first one lug nut, then the other. She started to speak, but her voice failed her on the first try. "It . . . it must've been a prank. They probably thought it would just fall right off."

"Probably." He looked into her eyes, then lowered his gaze to her lips. They were full and naturally pink, and he had the worst urge to touch them with the same two fingers that had flirted with her palm.

"I don't think anyone wanted to hurt you." He was looking at her differently now. The heat from his eyes made her mouth go dry, and she had to keep talking. "I think it was just a prank. Don't you?"

"Please don't ask me questions when you know I don't have any answers," he said quietly. "I hate that." He hated the fact that he was clenching his fists against the urge to touch her. The lug nuts cut into his hand.

"I think it was just a prank," she said again.

"I think I'd better see if I can get the damn tire back on the pickup." Before you read my mind, he thought. He figured his close brush with death must have triggered this suddenly urgent lust for... life.

"Do you have enough tools?" she called after him as he ambled back down the hill.

He laughed as he stood the tire on edge and started rolling it. "I sure have," he sang out. "All I'll ever need."

Once Sage had the pickup on the road again, he pulled the crumpled paper from his pocket and smoothed it out in the center of the steering wheel. "Accidents happen," the penciled note warned. "Don't interfere with free enterprise, Parker. It's the American way."

Red Calf, South Dakota, was a hole in the Badlands' wall. Megan drove past Floyd's Tavern, allowing herself a quick glance at the single car parked in front to assure herself that there were no crying children inside. She told herself that she wouldn't trust any meat that came from Floyd's Foods, the clapboard building that stood next door. The windows on both structures were covered with bars. She wondered who was being locked out. The town looked pretty dead.

A phone call to Pete Petersen and a little research on Pete's part had turned up the information she'd needed to attend a Medicine Wheel meeting. Sage had invited her, and something in the back of her mind wouldn't let the idea fade away. There was nothing wrong with caring, she told herself. But she wanted to care from an enlightened point of view. She'd come here to be enlightened.

The size of the Red Calf Community Center said something about the size of the community. A hundred people might have been able to crowd inside—if most of them were small. The sign taped to the door announced that the Medicine Wheel meeting was in progress and that anyone was welcome to attend. According to the sign, Megan was half an hour late, but Pete had said 8:00 p.m. She dreaded walking in late, but she opened the door and stepped inside.

A single bright, bare bulb in the ceiling illuminated a small circle of people, who turned in their folding chairs at the sound of the door. Megan searched for a familiar face and felt a rush of relief when she found one.

"Join us, Megan." Sage got up and offered his seat. "I'll get another chair."

"I'm sorry to interrupt," she began as she took a tentative step toward the chair. "I thought...I was told the meeting started at eight."

Sage flipped another chair open and pushed it into the circle, telling her again with a glance at the chair he'd vacated that she should sit down. "You must have seen one of the posters. We're starting earlier now."

She'd changed clothes since he'd seen her at work. He watched her smooth her pale blue skirt along the backs of her thighs as she sat down. A wide leather

belt the color of her skirt made her look wasp-waisted,
and he noticed for the first time that her ears were
pierced. When she turned to look up at him, he saw
the flash of blue stones. She'd done something extra
to her hair, and he noted signs of makeup. Then he
remembered that he was still standing, and he joined
the circle.

"We're all here because we want to make our lives
over without alcohol or drugs," Sage explained. "You
don't have to tell us anything. You've joined us.
You're part of the circle. As the night passes, you're
welcome to share what you will."

"Would I be breaking a confidence if I explained
our—" Her hand fluttered between them. "How I
know you?" From the flat look in his eyes, she could
tell that she'd already said the wrong thing.

"Not at all." Let's get our disclaimers out first, he
thought.

"I'm a highway engineer," Megan offered to the
group. "We're working on a project just west of here.
Sage—" She smiled, first at him and then at them.
"Sage has just been promoted to construction supervisor." No one smiled back, and she realized that she
had yet to tell them anything they didn't know, and,
so far, they weren't impressed.

"I don't have a problem, really," she went on hesi-
tantly. "Not a *personal* problem, anyway."

"How very fortunate for you."

She looked quickly at Sage and saw that he was
amused. "I mean I don't drink—much." He knew
damn well what she meant!

"Neither do I." One corner of his mouth hinted at a smile.

"I know that. I understand that." She looked at the ceiling, casting about for help. "I'm going about this all wrong."

"You don't have to protect yourself here, Megan. That's the beauty of the circle. Just tell us what's bothering you."

"Nothing," Megan said quickly. "I just want to learn. I want to know what kinds of things bother you...people." She looked around her and counted thirteen expressionless faces. Not a lucky number, she thought.

"I'll tell you something that bothers me," an older woman said. "Tourists. People who want to drive around in our backyards and then drive off to tell their friends about what it's like in Red Calf."

The woman's tone suggested no more emotion than her wrinkled brown face betrayed. Megan wanted to run. She glanced at Sage, but he was staring at the floor. "I'm not here because of curiosity," she said quietly. "A couple of the men on the crew...our—" Again she gestured to indicate that she and Sage were in this together. "*Our* crew. Members of your community, I believe—well, they have a problem with drinking. That is, they *seem* to have a problem with drinking."

"A problem that interferes with their work?" Sage asked without looking up.

"Yes." She looked around the room again as her fear began to take a backseat to her cause. "We had to fire one of the men, and I hated to see that happen.

He was a good worker before he started drinking again, and I'm sure he needed his job."

"Anybody else here need his job?" Sage asked, and there was a round of chuckling. "Most of these people don't have jobs, Megan. There aren't too many around."

"I know. That's why I'm concerned when I have to fire someone." She looked around quickly again. No one was looking at her. No one seemed to be listening, and she felt driven to regain their attention. "It seems like such a waste when a man is good at his job, and then, just because of alcohol, he's—"

"You're talking about my husband."

Megan turned toward the voice and recognized the woman with the beautiful black hair. "I'm sorry," Megan said. "I didn't mean—"

"Sage fired him, not you."

Megan's back stiffened. "Sage has his job to do, too."

"Jackie stopped coming to Medicine Wheel," Regina said. "He stopped going to work every day, and he deserved to be fired. Now he's stopped coming home at night."

"I'm sorry," Megan said again.

"Being sorry for him only makes him worse," Regina said. "Don't be sorry for him. He can get drunk on pity the same as he gets drunk on wine."

"But if he had his job, surely—"

"What we're telling you, Megan, is that the job was a small part of Jackie's loss," Sage told her. "He has to get his soul back before he can work again."

He looked at her now, and in his eyes she saw his acceptance of her presence, of her concern, of her fumbling attempt to understand. "Is there anything I can do?" she asked.

"You can pray," said the older woman who had spoken before. "For yourself, and for the rest of us, to whatever god you believe in."

That wasn't what Megan had had in mind. She looked to Sage for a better answer. "I think awareness is important," she explained. "For an employer, a supervisor. There must be something we can do to make it easier to... to adjust."

She didn't understand old Bessie's answer because she didn't understand Medicine Wheel, Sage thought as he nodded patiently. "Awareness is a good thing," he said. "So be aware that you can make it easy for a drunk to go on doing what he's doing. You can never make it easy for him to change."

"If somebody goes in for treatment, try to hold his job for him," said one man. "When I got out, I didn't have much to go back to. But I had this group." His mouth opened in a gap-toothed grin. "I'll have a job when Regina and Tootsie open their store."

"We've bought a house for it now," Regina announced. There was a low murmur of approval. "The White Shields' house. They're moving to Pine Ridge."

Conversation turned to plans for bringing grocery prices down in Red Calf. Floyd's was the only store, and, because the town was so isolated, he charged outrageously for food.

"Jackie borrowed money from Uncle Floyd again, and Floyd tried to get me to pay it," Regina complained. "You should see the interest he's got tacked on!"

"That's Jackie's debt," Sage reminded her. "You worry about opening up that store."

"I'll help you paint it."

"We'll need to knock out some walls."

"You guys can live upstairs."

"I know where you can get one of those big freezers for next to nothing."

The meeting had gone well. Sage lay across his bed from corner to corner and stared at the ceiling that curved three feet above his head as he played the meeting over in his mind. Jackie's relapse was a loss, but these things happened. The group members put it in perspective as they planned their course. Close down the bar and build a new store. Individual recovery would lead to community recovery. Ollie Walks Long had gone to Fort Meade. The group would have his house fixed up for him when he got back. They would clean it up and paint it, put new screens on the windows. It was important to have a decent place to live. Not fancy, but decent. You had to start someplace, and that was a good place to start. Jackie would come back, Sage decided, and they would help him start again, too.

Sage reached across the bed and groped for the switch on the little oscillating fan that whirred in the darkness next to him. He turned it up as high as it would go and promised himself that one day he would sleep in an air-conditioned bedroom again. He propped his head on his elbow and turned his face toward the hot breeze. Hell, just a bedroom would be nice. The back end of a fifteen-foot trailer could hardly be called a bedroom. He'd had a bedroom once, with an air conditioner in the window, but there had been too many times when that room had heated up even with the air on full blast. God, how the two of them had argued.

He remembered how pretty she'd been when she was seventeen. Riva Maxon. All he remembered about her from those days was that she had long blond hair, and she could do one hell of a spread-eagle at the end of a cheer. He'd gone to an Indian boarding school in Nebraska, and she'd gone to public school. She hadn't cheered for his team, but he'd soon had her cheering for him. She'd planned to go to college, but he'd changed her plans. He rodeoed in the summer, and she'd followed the circuit and learned all about cowboys. She'd had quite a teacher.

He was driven then, and he'd pushed hard—for thrills, for quick intensity, for sex on demand. To this day he didn't know what devil it was that had eaten at him so voraciously from the inside out. He had never been able to get enough of anything. He'd always wanted more. Drinking made him powerful and glib, made the women fun and easy, made the risks and the close calls seem like the best part of living. For a time he'd led a charmed life. He'd gotten by. He'd smashed the front fender, but he hadn't wrecked the car. He'd caught hell for flirting, but he hadn't gotten caught cheating. He'd paid most of his bills. But he hadn't catapulted himself high enough. Each time he'd come down, he seemed to find himself one rung lower, and he'd needed a closer call, a greater thrill, a bigger bottle, to get himself back up there again.

Just the memory made him sweat with fear. He edged closer to the fan and tried to replace those dark images with something else. Something that made him feel good. Megan. Clean, fresh hair that left the soft down on the back of her neck exposed. Clear-eyed innocence and courage. It had taken courage to do what she'd done tonight. At one point he'd thought she was going to bolt, but she'd stayed. She was a bona fide caretaker, sure as hell, but there was hope for her. She'd been willing to listen. And when she'd sat down in that chair and turned her face up to him, she'd looked so pretty that she'd made his insides turn to slush.

He commended himself for remembering that look on her face above all else. He'd spent hours wondering about her legs, and he'd finally gotten a look at them. They were nice, but it was her face that stuck fast in his thoughts. He couldn't remember when he'd given a woman's face such a big piece of his mind.

Yes he did. He remembered Riva's face when it wasn't pretty anymore. He remembered how she'd looked with her eyes narrowed and her lips thin and white as she spat obscenities at him. He wondered how he'd looked as he matched her curse for curse. Had he ever loved her? Was he capable of giving love? If he'd ever loved anyone, he didn't remember what it felt like. No, that wasn't true. He'd loved his children. God, he wanted to believe he'd always loved his two children. But he'd hurt them. He'd catered to himself and his addiction at their expense.

Sage rolled onto his back and studied the metal seams in the ceiling again. He didn't want to hurt anyone else. He didn't want to turn anyone else ugly. His pain was his, and he didn't anesthetize himself anymore. Losing his children would always hurt, but he didn't bottle it up anymore. He admitted it. He'd hurt them, and he lived with that pain. He would do what he could for the others who lived with the same kind of pain, and he would do his damnedest not to cause any more.

Brenda and Tommy. She was twelve now, and he was nine. It had been six years since Riva had left him and taken the kids. She'd remarried, and she wanted him to pay his child support and stay out of their lives. His letters were usually returned unopened, but not all of them. Some must have slipped through. He just wanted the kids to know that he cared. That was all. He didn't want to screw anything up for them, but it didn't hurt to care. Smiling to himself, he wiped the sweat off his chest with the corner of the sheet. It didn't hurt to care. That sounded like something Megan might say. He believed she did care about Jackie and Gary—maybe even himself. Well, if she let herself get too deeply involved, she would soon find out how much it hurt to care.

Damn, he wished they would answer his letters. With a groan, he turned his face toward the wall. If they would just send him a picture. . . .

Chapter 5

Terry Haynes wasn't satisfied with his assignment. Out of the corner of his eye Sage had watched Haynes use his boot heel to dig a hole in the soft ridge of clay base that the blade had left along the edge of the new road. Sage flipped the metal cover over his clipboard and waited while the rest of the crew headed for the equipment. He figured he and Haynes were about due.

"I want the overtime on the oiler," Haynes announced, his colorless eyes aglow with the bravado he'd been working himself up to during Sage's brief talk with the crew.

"You worked overtime last week," Sage reminded him quietly. There wasn't much Sage liked about Haynes. He was sloppy, both in his personal habits and his work. Sage didn't like the tobacco stains on the wiry young man's scraggly blond mustache, nor the little bits of tobacco between his teeth, nor his off-color sense of humor. Moreover, he didn't like the way the man handled the oiler. Sage had suggested, instructed and reprimanded, but Haynes knew it all. "I'm turning the oiler over to Archambault and putting you on the ground for a while."

Haynes shoved his hands in his back pockets and spat brown juice into the grass. "I'm going to file a complaint."

"That's your right." Sage turned to walk away.

"I don't much care for the way you take care of your Indian friends first, Parker."

Sage mentally counted through the single digits as he turned back slowly. "I don't much care for the way you run the oiler. I told you how I wanted it done, and you chose not to listen."

"I don't know who the hell you think you are, Parker." Haynes shifted his weight from one foot to the other and stuck out his chin, adding emphasis to the obscene bulge beneath his lower lip. "You go from labor to foreman overnight. What do you know about oiling? How many jobs you been on? They got some kinda Indian preference with state jobs now?"

In his head, Sage saw his fist connect with Haynes's mouth, splattering blood and brown slime all over that seedy mustache. He gripped the clipboard tightly in his right hand. "You're on the ground, or you're on your way back to wherever you come from, Haynes."

"You got an in with Krueger. Everybody knows that. And McBride—"

"File your complaint." Sage turned on his heel, his gut churning as he headed toward a big yellow steam-

roller, the only piece of equipment that wasn't moving at the moment. The roar of powerful diesel engines
filled his ears, and he fastened his mind on the noise.
He associated the sound with ripping out and packing down, and he needed to get his hands on the con-
trols. He needed to substitute the work for ripping
Haynes's teeth out of his mouth and packing them
down his throat.

Megan had spent the first part of the week in Pierre
at the highway department office. It had been good to
get back to her apartment for a few days. Staying in a
Hot Springs motel for the better part of the summer
was part of the highway engineer's territory, and she
didn't mind it. She wasn't a homebody. Sometimes she
wondered why she even needed her own apartment,
but the answer to that question came quickly. The
other choice was having a home base with her parents.

It was late afternoon when she climbed the steps to
the office. She'd toured the site, and she planned to
pick up some charts and head for Hot Springs. The
project was going well. Krueger was pleased with the
progress they were making, and he was especially
pleased with her positive report on Sage's job perfor-
mance. He'd long believed in Sage's potential, and he
liked being right about people.

Sage pulled up in front of the office soon after she
did. She smiled when she heard the old blue pickup's
engine refuse to die even after he'd shut it off. She
wondered if he did his own tune-ups, and if he did,

when he would ever find the time. She knew he was burning the candle at both ends these days.

Black dirt ringed his eyes where his sunglasses had been, and Megan was reminded of a raccoon. Sage tossed the glasses on the desk and pulled the blue bandanna off his head. It left a marked crease in his hair, which he ruffled with impatient hands.

"How's life in the big city?" he asked in lieu of greeting her with a hello.

"Not as exciting as it is out here," she said, smiling. "It looks good."

"What looks good? Your road?"

"My road." She liked the idea, and she gave a quick laugh. "It's taking shape. This time next year, there'll be traffic on it."

Sage unrolled the bandanna and wiped his face with it. He'd spent the day fuming over Haynes. Ordinarily he might have been able to let the incident go, but he was tired. He was just too damned tired to reason with himself. He knew his limits.

"Look, Megan—" He stuffed the bandanna in his back pocket and sat on the edge of his desk. "I want out of this job. I want my old job back."

Megan's face dropped. "Why?"

"This isn't my kind of thing. I'm a rancher who works construction to make ends meet. I don't like ordering people around."

Megan pushed the charts aside and sat on her desk, facing him. "There's always an adjustment period, Sage. The crew is coming around. They're beginning to see you as their supervisor instead of one of them." You can't make the changes any easier, he'd told her.

But she still believed there was a way to help with the adjustment. "You're doing a wonderful job. Bob says—"

"I don't care what Bob says." He worked to control his tone, to keep it even. He wanted her to listen to *him* now, not to Bob. He had something to tell her. "I can't do this anymore. I don't *want* to do this anymore."

"Why not?"

He gauged the look in her eyes and decided she might be listening. "I've got a temper," he confessed quietly. "When somebody mouths off to me, I get knots in my gut. I don't want to lose it, Megan." He met her gaze, and it made his eyes sting. He glanced away. "I've got my temper under control now, and I don't want to lose it."

"Did something happen today?"

"Yeah." He hadn't talked to anybody since the incident. She was right; the crew members no longer regarded him as one of them. He couldn't talk to Randy or Gary or any of the rest of them about one of their own. She was all he had, and he wanted to tell somebody, just to get it out. "I took Haynes off the oiler, and he didn't take it too well."

"How did you handle it?" she asked.

"I handled it okay." He frowned a bit as he reconsidered. "I handled it better than okay, but that isn't the point. I don't want to handle stuff like that at all."

"Nobody does. But you did it because that's what you're getting paid to do." She felt compelled to move closer. She stopped only a foot from his desk. "Don't quit, Sage," she implored. "Show them what you can do."

He saw the fire in her eyes, and he tipped his head back and gave a short bark of mirthless laughter. "Show who?" he demanded. "The crew? The highway department? Who?" He came to his feet, and she followed him with her eyes, lifting her chin as he rose above her. "I'm not out to prove what a 'good Indian' I can be. I'm not out to be a 'super success story.'"

"That isn't what I meant," she said evenly.

"You know, you have a lot of trouble with saying things you don't mean. Who am I supposed to make this big effort for? You?"

"Yourself. Your...your..." She gestured helplessly.

"Don't say 'my people,' or you'll blow what's left of my patience all to hell." She looked at him through widening eyes as she closed her mouth. "Wise move," he told her, then turned toward the window. He needed space. "I know I help fill a minority quota. I can live with that, because I also know I can move as much damn dirt as any man. Beyond that, I don't have any point to prove."

"I'm filling a quota, too," Megan told him quietly. "I was given this project because the department had been accused of sex discrimination."

He turned just enough so that he could see her face. "Who made the accusation?"

"I did. When I asked for this project, Bob Krueger went out on a limb for me."

"So we're both tokens." With a nod he turned to the window again. "And that scrawny little buzzard is up there leaping from one limb to the next. I supposed you're anxious for me to pan out as foreman for his sake."

"Bob took a stand. I don't see how we can allow ourselves to fail him."

"Fail *him*?" Sage faced her and shook his head. "Uh-uh, lady, don't lay that one on me. You wanted to prove a point, and you did it. You gained some ground for women. That's fine. If you're looking to move from sexism to racism now, you're gonna have a little trouble. You're white."

"That's not fair!" Megan took a step closer as her pulse shifted into higher gear. "I've seen what you can do, Sage, and I'm only suggesting that you take the bull by the horns and do it."

"Have you ever taken a bull by the horns?" The wide-legged stance she took as she folded her arms and glared in response to his question made him laugh again. "Not literally, right? I have, and let me tell you, it gives you a rush of power. Just like the one *you* get from trying to fix things for people."

"What are you talking about? I'm not trying to fix anything. I recommended you for this job be-cause...because, like it or not, you were right for it."

"Did you go up to Pierre and let them all know what a great choice you'd made?"

"No."

"How the Indian boy you hand-picked was mak-ing good?"

"You're hardly a boy."

"Yeah, but I was hand-picked to carry your banner, wasn't I?" She stood her ground as he edged closer, the volume of his voice on the rise. "Wasn't I, Megan? How many causes can one little wisp of a woman push for, anyway?"

They stared at one another for a moment, both wondering how much of what they'd hurled at one another was truth and how much was pure frustration. Finally, Megan turned and walked away.

"I'd rather you wouldn't quit," she said. "But if you're determined to do it, do it in writing."

At her back, she heard the door close quietly.

If the tire was going to go or the pickup was destined to overheat, Sage figured this was the time for it to happen. Careening down the gravel hill, he took pleasure in plowing up a billowing wake of dust. He felt as though the top of his head was about to blow. The lady was using him, sure as hell. He'd tried to level with her, and she'd given him some guidance counselor's pep talk. She'd sooner talk than hear something that didn't fit into her master plan.

He felt cut off. He wasn't part of the family. He wasn't part of the crowd. He wasn't even part of the crew anymore. The one person on the job that he should have been able to talk to had told him everything was really terrific. This was the way it was supposed to be, according to her. He would get used to it, just the way he'd gotten used to the other ties that had been cut. Used to it, hell! Adjust? He would have liked nothing better than to adjust her high and mighty little nose a few pegs lower.

He was pushing too hard. The pickup fishtailed, and he caught himself enjoying the moment of peril before he managed to align the front end with the back again. No, he was *being* pushed, he told himself, and he needed to push back. Purely on impulse, he reached for the glove compartment. His hand froze when he felt the heat of the metal button under his finger. The glove compartment was locked, and the keys were in the ignition. He kept that little bottle sealed and locked up tight.

God help him, he was reaching for an anesthetic on an impulse from the past. That's all over, he reminded himself. Four years past. He felt clammy, nearly sick. Staring hard at the road, he passed his fingers over his forehead, and they came away wet.

Slow down, he told himself. Breathe deeply, slow down, keep driving, and let these minutes tick by one at a time.

Chapter 6

He had the weekend to cool off. Sage put road construction on the back burner that Saturday morning and busied his hands and his heart with other labor. It might have been *her* road, but this house was his. He'd resisted shortcuts and detours, and he was doing it right this time. The only parts he hadn't been able to handle himself so far were drawing the blueprints, pouring the basement and raising the roof beams. Though the design was his, he'd paid an acquaintance to do the prints. He'd hired a cement contractor, and Medicine Wheel members had helped him raise the wall frames and the heavy ceiling beams that would be exposed when the house was finished.

He'd chosen the site carefully. The cabin that had been here once was where the seeds of his life had been planted. His taproot was there. Taproots grew deep in

prairie sod. In times of drought, they grew even deeper
and clung tenaciously to the heart of the earth. Sage
knew his was there, in this spot where his family's
cabin had stood. The structures they'd built in the interim had been without foundation, and they'd disappeared. Though the cabin was gone, too, it had left
him with good memories. He was determined to reconnect himself with that taproot. Without it, he'd
withered pathetically during life's inevitable periods of
drought.

Sage surveyed his work as he organized his tools.
The studs and rafters cast long shadows in the slanted
rays of the morning sun. It was beginning to look a lot
like a real house. He'd given himself good-sized rooms
because he was tired of being cramped, and there were
two extra bedrooms. There would come a day when
his letters would be answered, and Brenda and Tommy
would each have a room when they came to visit after
school got out for the summer. It was a dream he'd
come to cherish. He wondered whether Brenda still
loved horses as much as she had when she was a little
girl, and whether Tommy ever sucked his thumb anymore. Every time his mother had plucked it out of his
mouth, the dark-eyed little boy had waited until she'd
turned her back, and then he'd shoved it right back in.

Sage tied his carpenter's apron over the wide leather
belt that rode low on his hips and admonished himself to get to work. A man could drive himself crazy
wondering about some things. He climbed the ladder
to the roof. He had a subfloor, and all the wall frames
and partitions were in place. Once he finished this
part, he could say he had a roof over his head. By

winter he hoped to have the shell finished and the shingling done. If he could afford to put in a wood-stove, he could work inside during the winter. He was collecting a paycheck now that might cover those things—but only if he continued as foreman.

From the top of his roof he could see the edge of the world. To the north the rows of cottonwoods, silver-leafed Russian olives and thick wild plum bushes provided shelter from the winter wind. The great plains rolled to the south like a dun-colored blanket, with green and yellow beadwork applied deep within the nap. Flat-topped buttes ringed the horizon, and the sky was gloriously high, wide and blue.

Sage hummed to himself as he worked. The re-sounding, rhythmic tap of his hammer was his ac-companiment, and the song was one he'd learned recently from a medicine man. It was a song to sweat by, the old man had told him, and Sage was doing just that. His body was purging itself. Yesterday's anger was dissipating, and he gave voice to the sense of re-lief that brought him as he basked bare-chested in the morning sun.

A bright yellow highway department pickup slowed at the approach to his rutted, gravel driveway. Sage willed the quick tie-up in the pit of his stomach to go away as he braced himself on one knee and stretched his torso. He watched the vehicle draw near. What was she doing there?

Megan stepped around a stack of plywood and squinted at a rafter that pointed the way to the sun. "Sage? Are you up there?"

The head that rose over the ridge of the roof caused an eclipse. His face was shadowed, and the sun's rays seemed to crown him. "Morning," he greeted her. "Taking the scenic tour?"

"Not exactly." She stepped closer to the ladder. "I came to see you. Could you use a short break?"

"I was just on my way down."

She watched him negotiate the ladder. He wore vintage high-top basketball shoes and well-worn jeans, and his hair gleamed blue-black in the sun. "I won't keep you long," she promised.

"That's too bad." He skipped the last three rungs and hopped to the ground. "I'd just about decided I wanted to be kept." He wiped the sweat from his brow with the back of his wrist and gave her a slow smile. "On the job."

"Really?" It was the one piece of news she hadn't anticipated. "I guess I can put away my speech, then."

"You came prepared with a speech?" Still smiling, he hooked his thumbs in his belt. "I've gotta hear this."

"I'll just skip to the last line. I'm sorry for anything I said yesterday that sounded patronizing."

"Patronizing?" He considered it and nodded. "Yeah, that's a good word for it."

"The truth is that I need a good foreman on this project, and you're good. You've let the crew know what's expected of them, and you don't let anyone slide by. They all respect you, Sage, including Haynes. They've all seen you work. They know you're not asking them to do anything you haven't done yourself. That's why you're right for this job. No other reason."

"All that was part of the last line?"

She smiled. "So I backtracked a little. The apology seemed a little naked."

"I'm sorry I flew off the handle. The truth is, I was mad." He shrugged. "I got over it."

"Haynes is a hothead," Megan assured him. "He's probably over it by now, too."

Sage laughed. "I've been called a hothead myself."

"But you've got it under control now," she reminded him.

"I'm working on it." He untied his carpenter's apron and laid it on top of his tool box. "How about some coffee?"

"I really don't mean to keep you from your work." She looked up at the skeletal structure. "And this looks like quite a project. You're building this all by yourself?"

"I've had a little help on occasion." He moved to the stack of plywood sheets. "Just let me rack up another load of lumber, and then I'll show you around."

The plywood rack leaning against the roof looked like another ladder, but it had two wedges nailed halfway up, which held a supply of plywood and put it within reach of a man on the roof. "That's ingenious," Megan said as she watched him lift a sheet into place.

"It's an extra pair of hands." When he'd filled the rack, he motioned for her to follow him through the opening that would become the front door. "Give me a woman's opinion of the floor plan."

Megan stepped across the threshold. "I'm better equipped to give you an opinion on the design of your driveway."

"You wanna help me rearrange the ruts?"

"There's one place that angles a little too far to the left." She indicated a sharp curve with her hand as she passed under the header of the doorway between the living room and the kitchen. Her pink sleeveless top and blue jeans skimmed her body as though they were all of a piece. The thick rubber soles of her running shoes emphasized the smallness of her feet. He stood in the middle of a rough lumber kitchen and saw nothing but delicacy as he watched her come toward him.

"It lacks good engineering," he said absently.

"So what's this?" She waved a hand at the rafters. "The gym?"

"The kitchen. Dining area over here. Nice view of the road, so you can see who's coming and throw on some coffee. Exposed beams. Patio door. The deck comes later." He drew pictures in the air. Everything but the view and the beams would come later. He hadn't bought any glass yet.

She imagined a redwood deck where he indicated that it would be on the tree-lined side of the house. "When did you start?"

"Three years ago." He laughed at her look of surprise. "It may be a lifelong project. I don't have any credit."

"You mean you're doing this without a loan?"

"I've had loans. I got behind on my payments, and the creditors sold everything on the place that was portable, even the house. It didn't cover what I owed, but they divvied up the money and went away satisfied." He leaned on a future windowsill and watched as the breeze made the tall grass ripple. "My land—the part that I actually own—was in trust, so they didn't try to mess with it."

"You mean because your ranch is part of the reservation?" she asked.

He nodded. "It's my land, but the trustee relationship between the federal government and the tribe makes it pretty complicated to use Indian land as collateral. So—" He sat against the windowsill and faced her with a smile that surprised her. "I lost the leased land, too, but I've got most of that back now. I lost everything but the land I actually had title to."

"It was precious to you," she concluded solemnly. "Part of your heritage."

He told her what she wanted to hear. "We call the earth Grandmother." She nodded as though she understood thoroughly, and he wanted to burst out laughing because her gullibility delighted him, but he knew she would misunderstand. He held it down to a twitching grin. "There was a time when I would have sold Grandmother in her wheelchair for another ticket on the merry-go-round. But there were federal restrictions that wouldn't let me go quite that far."

It was hard to imagine the man in front of her being the man he'd described. He was exaggerating. He was being dramatic, she decided, even though he showed no sign of self-pity. "If you weren't close to the land, then why all this?" Her gesture encompassed the house and all that surrounded it. "You're obviously sinking every penny you make back into this place."

"Almost," he agreed. "I'm a rancher. Rebuilding my life means rebuilding this place. When I was drinking, booze was the buffer between me and everything I cared about, so I wasn't really close to anything. Of the things that I cared about, the land is what I have left. It's where I have to start." He chuckled. "Everything else had legs."

He moved away from the windowsill and jerked his chin toward the rest of the house. "C'mon. We haven't finished the tour. Bedroom...bathroom... bedroom... *my* bedroom. Get this!" He walked through a wall and gestured with a flourish. "Room for a king-size bed." She looked a little startled, and he laughed as he pointed between the wall studs at the tiny trailer on the other side of the driveway. "That's what I'm sleeping in now."

"Looks pretty small." She leaned her shoulder against the door frame and folded her arms. "What about stock? You can't buy cattle without credit."

"Who says?" Pride glistened in his eyes as he rested his hands on his hips. "I've got fourteen stock cows and five horses now. And they're mine, free and clear. I'll sell the calves in the fall and buy bred heifers." She looked skeptical. "Hey, I've got plenty of time. I'm only thirty-four. When I was twenty-four, I thought time was running out on me. Now I've got all the time in the world. By next spring I might have twenty cows and all the outside walls up, but if I only have eighteen cows and a roof—" he shrugged "—I'll still be doing what I want to do. You like horses?"

"Yes, very much." He gave the familiar chin-jerk toward the corral. Then he stepped between two wall studs and hopped to the ground. When Megan got to the edge of the subfloor he was waiting to help her down.

He could see that there was an automatic protest on the tip of her tongue. His assistance wasn't necessary. Their eyes met, and she read the message. The offer of his hand was a chance to touch, just briefly. The choice was hers. He reached for her, and she put her hands in his. It was like thrusting them quickly in front of a fire. The rest of her body was suddenly flushed with envy as she indulged only her hands. When her feet were firmly planted on the ground, she tipped her chin up, and they made a silent pact to linger over the indulgence a moment longer.

A stout sorrel gelding stood in one corner of the corral, with a brown and white pinto mare and her colt in another. The colt stole the show. His springy white mane and sassy flag of a tail were set off by well-defined patches of dark brown. He pranced circles around his mother as Sage stepped onto one rail, swung his leg over the top of the fence and sat down. Megan clambered up one rail at a time.

"I was stretching it a little," he said, grinning down at her. "I've got four horses and a colt, but he's one hell of a colt."

"He's beautiful," she agreed. "I think he counts as a horse."

"The first thing I did was repair the corrals and put up the pole barn. I had a prefab metal barn that was auctioned off. I used wood this time, because it's warmer in the winter and cooler in the summer.'' She seemed interested, so he continued. "Maybe it's a little like building a road. I need to see it take shape. I'm watching it rise from the dust, kind of like me—my own resurrection. I'd been sober for about a year when I came back out here and dug the first post hole. I'd been avoiding the place for three years, but I learned something that day about making a start." He remembered the day, and the tears he'd shed as he'd rammed the post hole digger into the ground, making a mark. Taking a step. His eyes searched the east end of the corral and found that benchmark. "One post. I came back the next day, and it was still there, so I knew I'd actually done it. I'd taken that first step."

"I admire your courage."

He looked at her and found that the complete sincerity in her eyes embarrassed him. "Courage, hell," he tossed off as he jumped down from the corral. "No more than it takes anybody else to put one foot in front of the other. I only had one direction left to go, and that was up." He cocked his head to one side as he looked up at her. "I promised coffee, didn't I? How about some lunch?"

In three steps, Megan was down on the ground beside him. "I really didn't mean to keep you from your work."

"I have to eat sometime." He made a point of surveying her slim figure. "You do, too, and the eating establishments around here are few and far between. You can have a sandwich with me, or drive into Red Calf for frozen pizza at Floyd's Tavern."

"Which is closed."

"Damn, that's right!" Grinning broadly, he snapped his fingers. "A bunch of troublemakers shut him down. Guess it's sandwiches or starvation."

She returned his smile. "Sandwiches, then."

Her reply gave him a momentary feeling of buoyancy, and then he realized that he was taking her into the trailer. He hesitated at the foot of the small set of wooden steps. "There's not much room," he said. "And not much ventilation. It gets pretty hot and, uh, pretty cramped."

"I don't have much of a home, Sage. An apartment, just big enough to store some personal things." It was her turn to reach out to him. She laid a hand on his arm, then looked up at him. "I'm not even much of a cook, but I can spread mayonnaise."

"Should we eat in the dining room?" He nodded toward the new house, and his eyes twinkled in anticipation.

"Oh, yes, let's."

The trailer was, as promised, hot and cramped. Sage set the sandwich makings on the counter, and Megan put them together while he found canned soft drinks and potato chips to go with their meal. It felt good to get back outside, where the air was moving and space was unlimited. They sat cross-legged on the plywood subfloor, ate sandwiches and talked about the house. Sage explained his "master plan," and Megan complimented his design. "Three bedrooms is a lot for one person. Is there a chance that your family might come back to you?"

He shook his head. "My family belongs to somebody else now. My wife remarried, and she doesn't want any interference from me."

"If you're paying child support, you could probably insist on some—"

He shook his head and waved the suggestion away. "I'm not going to insist on anything. I'm hoping they'll give me a chance to redeem myself, but they have some pretty bad memories, and I can understand..."

"Were you . . . physically abusive?"

"No. I don't think so." He took a drink from the can he held in his hand, then gave her an unguarded look. His dark eyes became haunted. "I started having blackouts. I'd wake up with a godawful hangover and realize I'd lost a day somewhere. I had no idea where I'd been, or what I'd done."

"That's scary."

"Damn right it's scary. You have to try to get people to tell you what you did without letting them know you don't remember. I had a black eye once, and I never found out who gave it to me." He chuckled. "I think it was my brother." His smile faded as he continued to recall the bad times. He drew a deep breath and glanced toward the highway. "Once I found that I'd driven my daughter to school, and I didn't remember doing it." He looked at Megan. "I was dead drunk, and I was out on the road with that kid in the car."

It was her turn to glance away. She thought of the way Sage had held Regina's little boy, and she remembered her relationship with her own father—or lack of it. "My father drinks too much, too." The words were out before she'd thought about saying them.

He saw the startled look in her eyes and knew her betrayal of "the family secret" surprised her more than it did him. "Maybe that's why you have this concern for—"

"He's not an alcoholic," she hastened to add. "I guess I would say he's more a . . . a problem drinker."

"A problem drinker? What's that?"

"Well, he's never lost his job over it or anything. He doesn't fight, and he doesn't . . . you know . . . do anything really *bad*. . . ." She stared at the hole in the top of her soft drink can as she lifted her shoulders in a helpless shrug. "He just drinks too much sometimes. . . . *Most* of the time."

Sage knew he was watching her become, for the moment, the little girl she'd once been—the one who'd been told not to talk about her father's drinking. "It bothers you to see him drink?" he asked gently.

She smiled quickly and swept her hair back from her forehead as she squared her shoulders. She was a woman again. "I don't have to be around it anymore. I do think my mother should do something about him, though. He's getting too old to behave so foolishly."

"I wish my wife had done something about me, too." He chuckled, shaking his head at the beauty of the notion. "It would have been a hell of a lot less work for me if she'd just taken the bull by the horns—" he gave Megan a lopsided grin along with the expression "—and made me quit drinking. Maybe she could have sewn my mouth shut or something."

"Well, it's just…it's just so…" It just wasn't funny, and she refused to laugh about it. Instead she crushed the empty pop can with the heels of her hands. "It's good that you've done it for yourself. I admire you for it. You've started the recovery group, and you're building this place from scratch." She lifted her hands to indicate the work that surrounded them. "I just think it's wonderful."

She sounded a little like that school counselor giving him a pep talk again, but he knew that was to be expected. She'd put all her eggs into her professional basket. There she was sure, astute, determined to achieve. In her personal life, she wore blinders.

"What do you hear about Karl Taylor?" he asked as he lifted his soda can and judged he had about two more swallows left.

"I saw him when I was in Pierre," she told him. "I ran into him in the parking lot at the highway department."

"Did he say anything to you?"

"Some dumb comment about equal opportunity." Taylor had actually wondered whether Megan was giving Sage equal opportunity at the trap Taylor had accused her of baiting first for him. She'd ignored him. The idea that she would actually flirt with Taylor was ludicrous.

"You know that Floyd is Karl's brother," Sage said, and she nodded. "I think one of them might have had something to do with setting my tire up to fall off."

Her eyes widened. "Really?"

"Really," he echoed with a nod. "And if I'm right, then I think you need to be careful, too."

"Karl's been with the department for twenty years, at least. He's not going to jeopardize his job by trying to get back at me."

"No?" Sage lifted one eyebrow doubtfully. "I wouldn't bet on it, Megan. I'd stay clear of him."

"I'm sure Karl Taylor and I will be happy to stay clear of each other." She smiled. "I'm glad you've decided to stay on as foreman, Sage. You've made my job so much easier."

"Oh yeah?" She nodded. "Well, how about you making *my* job a little easier?" He stood up, and she followed suit, looking at him curiously. "Can you handle a hammer?" he asked as he headed for the tool box.

"Of course."

"How about heights?"

"No problem."

"Then if you're going to hang around here on my day off—" He tossed a hammer in the air, caught it by the head and offered her the handle. "—I'm gonna put you to work."

She smiled as she took the tool in her hand. "You mean I get to be on the crew?"

"You get to be the *whole* crew, since I seem to be stuck with the foreman's job."

"We'll see if I can stand working for you. Lead the way."

"You've gotta wear one of these." He handed her a canvas carpenter's apron that advertised Schultz Lumber, then reached for his leather one.

"An apron!" She laughed. "For this I spent four years in college?"

"And we'll be using these," he told her as he dipped into a box of eight-penny nails and added some to his own apron. "So fill up your pockets. This project is on a tight budget, so if you bend too many nails—" She dropped a couple from the handful she was loading into her apron, and she glanced up quickly. He gave her a teasing grin. "I'll keep you after five and make you straighten them out."

"Tyrant." She knelt to pick up the lost nails.

"You bet. That's why I'm so perfect for my job." He gestured toward the ladder. "You go up first, and I'll hold the ladder steady."

He watched her step carefully from the ladder to the plywood sheathing that was already nailed in place. She turned, established her balance on the pitched roof and looked out over the prairie. "You sure you're okay up there?" he asked.

"I'm fine." She shaded her face with her hand. "What a gorgeous view!"

The breeze lifted her honey-colored hair back from her face, and she reminded him of a fine-carved figure on the bow of a sailing vessel. "I'll say."

Chapter 7

I guess Regina finally reported Jackie missing.''

Sage pushed the button under his thumb, but he hesitated in opening the pickup door as he turned a puzzled look toward Gary Little Bird. "I thought he'd run off to North Dakota."

"That's what Regina thought. He's got relatives up there, and that's where he always goes. But she got hold of them, and they said he never showed up there."

Sage left the door ajar as he turned around. It was quitting time, and crew members were heading for their vehicles. Out of the corner of his eye he noted that Gary's news had caught Megan's attention. She, too, had paused on her way to her pickup.

"It's been at least a week since he's been home," Sage reflected. "Nobody's seen him?"

"Well, the cops did some checking, and I guess Roger Makes War and Henry Beaver finally admitted they were with him Monday night."

Sage braced his hand on the top of the cab and peered at Gary with concern. "That's four days. Nobody's seen him since?"

Gary shook his head. "First they said they'd taken him home after a party and let him off near his house. Now they admit they're not exactly sure where they put him out of the car. He said something about going to work and told them to let him off." Gary shrugged. "They pulled over, and he got out. That was the last they saw of him."

"What time was that?"

Gary offered a feeble laugh. "Hell, Sage, they don't know. They were all pretty wasted. They figure sometime after midnight."

"And he said he was coming to work?" Megan asked as she joined the two men. "Poor Jackie."

Sage directed a sigh skyward. "Yeah," he said disgustedly. "Poor Jackie."

"Well, listen, I'd better be taking off." Gary shoved his hands in his pockets and took a couple of steps backward. "I'll let you know if I hear anything else." There was a note of pride in his voice as he explained to Megan, "My brother's a dispatcher at the police station, so I get all the news."

"Coming to work in the middle of the night," Megan mused as Gary walked away. "I wonder how far—"

"Oh, God, no." Sage closed his eyes as an olfactory recollection burst forth in his brain. Muttering a curse, he jerked on the pickup door and hopped in.

"Sage, what is it?"

Megan fastened both hands on the door handle, and he gave her a hard look through the half-open window. "Stay here. I'll be right back, so just stay here."

It had been somewhere between the construction site and the little town of Buffalo Gap. The pickup plowed furrows into the gravel as Sage pushed the pedal to the floor and tried to remember where he'd stopped to fix that flat on his way to work—when? Had it been Wednesday morning? How far down? The memory of the odor became sharper, and he began to feel queasy all over again. It wasn't only the smell. It was the strange feeling he'd had that the odor was beckoning him somehow. He'd ignored all but the fact that the stench was sickening, and he'd hurried to change the tire and move on.

He braked suddenly. There was nothing notable about the spot—no landmark to distinguish it from the rest of the four-strand barbed wire that separated miles of grassy prairie from miles of gravel road. But something appealed to him to stop there, and he knew instinctively what it was. He was attuned to it again. Wiser men than he would have cautioned him to resist this kind of eerie summons, but resisting wasn't possible this time. He left the pickup door standing open and cleared the roadside ditch with one long leap.

He ignored the approach of another vehicle as he negotiated the barbed wire, stretching two strands above his head and holding two down under his boot.

The stench was still in the air. Putrefying flesh. It should have been an animal, the carcass of something meant to live and die out there in the middle of nowhere. Sage knew it wasn't. He dreaded what he would find, but he ran unerringly toward it. Two ravens sprang from the grass, black wings aflutter as they pumped hard to gain height quickly.

Sage slowed down as he approached. A snatch of blue lay in the grass ahead. The thudding of his own heartbeat was the single encroachment on the vast quiet. His boots trampled the grass that had served as a shroud, and Sage stood before the gaping face of death and heard its bleak cry echo in his head.

"Christ," he whispered. He tipped his head back, repeating the petition as he watched the white wisp of a cloud slip by.

Megan gripped the steering wheel as she watched Sage make his discovery. She knew what it was, but her heart said no, it couldn't be. It couldn't happen, not like this. She eased herself from the pickup and approached the fence. Neither her hands nor her brain was functioning properly, and she tore the shoulder of her jumpsuit as she struggled to get through the fence. From a distance she saw Sage pass his hand over his face and take a step back, and her stomach twisted painfully. She began to run.

He turned when he heard the swishing grass, and when he saw her, he panicked. There were no conscious thoughts now—only an instinctive need to spare her. He ran like a man possessed and caught her, trapping her arms between them. She looked up at him, her eyes cold with fear.

"It's Jackie," he said. She saw that much of the color had drained from his face, and his eyes looked haunted and hollow. Whatever he had seen had done this to him. It made no sense, but she tried to pull away. "No," Sage barked. "You can't go over there."

"But—" Her face crumpled. "You mean he's been there...all this time?" He nodded solemnly, and she had no words. There were only the small sounds. "Oh...oh..."

Sage put his arm around her, and they started walking. He wouldn't allow her to see what he had seen. He was there to protect her...and Jackie. The living could share their grief, but the dead had a right to some privacy. Sage would shield Jackie's torn and bloated remains from the final indignity of being viewed.

Like a pair of automatons, they put one foot in front of the other. "How did you know?" she asked.

"I had a flat tire the other morning. I could smell...something dead. I assumed it was an animal."

"But then today..."

"Today I knew." *Today I heard him call me.*

"How could it have happened?" Megan asked as she put her arm around Sage's waist, hoping to return some measure of comfort.

"He must have passed out and died of exposure."

"But it's summer," she protested. "It hasn't rained this week, and it's not that cold at night."

"It can still happen," he said. "Any number of things could have happened. Something inside, like heart failure or alcohol poisoning. He could have gone into shock. He could have choked on his own vomit.''

"Oh, Sage..."

"He's dead. That's all that matters."

"But what about those two men who left him out here in the middle of nowhere?"

"I don't know." He shook his head and sighed heavily. "I don't know. All I know is that Jackie found the other way to get off the merry-go-round."

"The other way?"

"You either quit drinking or let it kill you."

Megan leaned against his side as they walked back to the road, and Sage adjusted his arm as they drew closer. "Did you tear this on the barbed wire?" She lifted her face with a blank stare. "Your shoulder's bleeding."

She turned her head to examine the shoulder he held close to his chest. His long fingers pulled the torn edges of fabric apart to expose the bleeding patch of skin. "It's nothing," she said. "Just a scratch."

"You'll need a tetanus shot. That stuff's probably rusty."

She lifted her gaze from the scratch to his eyes. She wondered how a slight injury like hers could mean anything in the face of what he'd just witnessed. The light in his eyes told her that it did. Blood meant life, and Jackie had bled the last of his. "I'll be all right," she promised as she tightened her grip on his waist.

It seemed fitting, if tragic, that another liquor license hearing would be held two days after Jackie's body had been discovered. Megan went to the council chambers on her own this time, and when she saw that the chair next to Sage was empty, she went to it and sat down. He looked up, and his face betrayed no surprise at seeing her there.

"Hi," he said simply.

"Hi." She tried to assess the activity in the room. The councilmen were getting coffee and shuffling through papers, and there were people milling around the room, moving chairs and talking. "Have they started yet?"

"Sort of. We're between issues at the moment."

"Will you be speaking?" He nodded as he watched the chairman, who was examining some papers. Megan noticed that Jackie's wife was sitting only a few chairs away. "How's Regina doing?" she asked quietly.

"Okay." Sage leaned forward and rested his elbows on his knees, a manila folder dangling from his hand.

Megan realized that Sage had his upcoming presentation on his mind, and she settled back to wait with him. There was a good deal of conversation going on around her, much of it concerning Jackie's death.

"They said the autopsy was inconclusive," a man behind her reported. "They said it was like examining two-week-old hamburger."

"No ears, that Jackie," a woman's voice said. "Last time he was in detox, the doctor told him his liver was gonna get him sooner or later."

"Rotten hamburger, rotten liver—what's the difference? When your time comes, what's left is just coyote bait anyway."

"Eeez, what a thing to say. He was only thirty-five."

"I'm out of cigarettes." The complaint was punctuated with a smoker's cough. "Ask Boo Boo if he's got any."

"We'll be eating potato salad over you pretty soon if you don't quit that smoking. Listen to you."

The woman leaned past Megan and tapped someone who was sitting just down from Sage. Megan glanced up, curious to see who Boo Boo was, and realized that Sage was watching her eavesdrop. She felt her face grow warm.

"They always have a lot of potato salad at the wakes around here," he explained. Then he laid a hand on her arm and inclined his chin toward the side door. Megan followed the direction of his gaze.

Floyd Taylor had slipped into the room, accompanied by his brother, Karl. Side by side, the two reminded Megan of a pair of bulldog bookends that had always sat on her father's desk and defied anyone to tamper with his papers. Karl took a careful survey of the room, and Megan felt his cold stare the moment he picked her out of the crowd.

As the meeting progressed the chairman expressed his condolences to Regina and invited her to be first to speak on the issue at hand. Regina's voice cracked as she read the statement she'd prepared. She said that it was too late for Jackie, but she didn't want alcoholism to kill his children. For that reason, she wanted tighter control over the sale of alcohol.

When Sage came to the microphone, he asked whether the councilmen had had time to study the information he'd presented to them at the last hearing. There were a few nods and several voices indicating the affirmative.

"Once again I've come before this council to remind you of your duty to look out for the welfare of the people you represent. If you've read those reports, then you know in your gut that Floyd Taylor's business and the way he conducts it are a hazard to our health."

Floyd came to his feet. "I object to that kind of talk, Mr. Chairman!" He pointed a beefy finger at Sage. "And I could get you for slander, Parker. You've got no business accusing me!" He addressed the chair again. "I sell a product. I don't tell people how to use it. Why don't you prohibit the sale of vanilla extract and varnish, too? And how about cough medicine? If people want to get drunk—"

"Sit down, Mr. Taylor," the chairman ordered in a calm voice. "Mr. Parker has the floor."

"We're going to bury a man tomorrow," Sage continued without sparing Taylor so much as a glance. "Jackie Flying Elk tried to quit. We all watched him. Some of us encouraged him, and some of us laughed and told him he'd never make it. He didn't. So when we put him in the ground tomorrow, we can think to ourselves that this is the way it is, and nothing's ever going to change. Or, like Regina, we can tell ourselves that this is not what we want for our children. We can make this decision for ourselves." He lowered his voice and stirred the silence. "We can say *no more* to Mr. Taylor's . . . product."

After the applause the discussion continued, but it was largely redundant and uninspiring after the impact of Sage's presentation. Once again the issue was tabled.

"Tabled!" Megan snapped as they stood to leave. "What kind of a decision is that?"

"It's a reprieve," Sage said quietly. "We don't have enough votes, but we're being given a little more time, thanks to Jackie."

"I want to speak to his wife." Megan searched the crowd and spotted the beautiful fall of black hair. She made her way to Regina's side and offered her hand as she'd seen the others do. It was not so much a handshake as a pressing of one palm against another. Megan expressed her sorrow, and Regina nodded with sad dignity.

"Have they brought him home yet?" Sage asked.

"They're taking him to the church basement," she said. "He should be there soon."

"I'll drive you over." He turned to Megan. "The funeral's tomorrow morning. I won't get to work until about one."

She nodded and pulled back from the conversation, watching the crowd split and move past them on either side. She knew she'd done what she could; she'd given moral support at the meeting, and she'd expressed condolences to Jackie's widow. It was time she left Sage to share Regina's grief. Her peripheral vision blurred as she fastened her attention on them.

When they moved toward the door, she followed, giving them space. She was an outsider, but somehow she couldn't bring herself to make a graceful exit. She had known Jackie, too, and she'd been concerned about him. She had been there when Sage had discovered his body. She felt that she had a part in this, although she wasn't sure what her part was. She was an outsider, she reminded herself, but she cared about what was going on here. Couldn't they see that?

Mentally she chided herself for her selfishness. Regina had lost her husband, and Sage had lost a friend. Megan shared no real part in their grief. They hardly noticed when she moved away and headed toward her pickup.

At the last moment Sage turned, smiled and said, "Thanks for coming."

Responding to her own needs, Megan found it impossible not to return the following morning. The small white frame church was packed with mourners. A man offered her one of the folding chairs that had been arranged behind the pews, and she was handed a hymnal. She opened the book and found that the hymns were in Lakota.

Sage was one of the six solemn-faced pall bearers. They were all dressed differently, none in the traditional dark suit. One wore a plaid Western shirt buttoned tightly around his neck and adorned with a beaded bolo tie. Another wore a white shirt with a leather vest, and a third was dressed in a dated beige suit. This was the first time Megan had seen Sage dressed up, and, although his light blue sport jacket and tan slacks might not have been deemed appropriate for the occasion in other circles, she saw that fashion was not the measure of anything here. One dressed in his best, whatever it might be, and came to mourn.

As she watched Sage perform his duties and then take a seat in the front row, Megan was struck unexpectedly by the sheer beauty of the man. It wasn't just the rich contrast between his white shirt and his brown skin, or the shiny fullness of his black hair, but it was the way he moved, the way he carried himself smoothly, without any ado. He did nothing to call attention to himself, yet he commanded it. There was a kind of serenity in his face that inspired serenity in the heart of one who watched him. There was solace in knowing that he had survived so much suffering, yet the serenity was still there.

The service alternated English with Lakota, and it spoke of Jackie's death as part of life. Megan recognized the tunes of familiar hymns, but it was as though each note were being pulled through a sieve by mournful voices in a language that tore at the soul without any translation. By the time she pulled her pickup into line at the end of the cortege, she felt that her heart had been wrenched beyond repair, but she was drawn up the hill for the finish, even so.

There was no hearse. The casket, draped in a red, white and blue star quilt, was unloaded from the back of a pickup. The six men carried it through a gate that was marked by two tall, white poles. Megan waited inside her pickup, watching the crowd file along the perimeter of the woven wire fence. Old women wore dark sweaters and tri-cornered scarves to keep the warm wind off their gray heads. Children let the tips of their fingers bounce along the woven wire squares as they followed along to the gravesite.

Megan climbed down from the pickup and brushed at the wrinkles in her navy blue skirt. Overhead the clouds were thick and gray and rushing quickly across the sky. She took her place at the end of the line and followed unobtrusively. She walked past graves that were simply marked, some with wooden crosses, some with small white frames of wood. There were a few headstones and a few faded plastic floral tributes. For the most part, this was prairie. It was buffalo grass, prickly pear cactus and purple South Dakota cone-flowers. And it was dust.

There were no blankets of fake grass to profane the earth that would receive Jackie's body. The casket was lowered by hand, and the ends of the ropes were dropped on top of it. As the mourners sang another hymn, Sage left the graveside and came to stand beside Megan. He saw the tears welling in her eyes, and he took her hand. Gratefully she hung on tight, for life was as dear at that moment as it had ever been.

When the last note of the hymn had drifted out over the grass, another sound took its place. It was Regina's keening—the high-pitched song of grief that only a woman's voice could carry and only a woman's heartbreak could produce. Her sorrow echoed in the hills while Sage and the other pall bearers filled the grave with earth.

"Why did you come?" Sage asked Megan in a hushed tone as he sat beside her in her pickup and watched the others drive away.

"I was with you when you found him." She glanced
over her shoulder at the fresh mound of earth behind
the fence. "I wanted to see him put to rest."

"Grief is one thing. Pity's another." She turned
back to him, and he saw a glint of pain in her ice-blue
eyes. He told himself to handle her carefully. "You
know that, don't you?"

"I've never witnessed the kind of grief I heard today. I'd thought maybe..." She glanced away again.
"Maybe people were disgusted with him...because of
the way he died."

"Were you disgusted with him?"

She shook her head quickly and looked down at her
hands. Tears burned in her throat again. "It must have
been a terrible way to die. Alone like that."

"What makes you think anyone else would come to
this hill today with feelings of disgust?"

She heard no malice in his voice and saw none in his
eyes, but his question sounded accusing. She wanted
to accuse him in return. "It just seemed that the man
was floundering so pathetically, and no one wanted
to... to..."

"To take care of him?"

His voice was soft, but she saw the challenge in his
eyes. She sought the words to meet it. "Some people
need to be taken care of... sometimes."

"Children do," he told her. "But if you treat a man
like a child, he's tempted to behave like a child. We've
been treated like children for a hundred years, Megan. It's damn tough to break the habit."

"You've been treated shamefully," she agreed. "I
know that. I don't want to be part of that. I want to be

open-minded and fair, and I want to try to...to make things right in whatever small way—''

''Make things right?'' He chuckled. ''How is one little white lady going to make things right?''

''In my own small way,'' she repeated, emphasizing each word. ''I cared about Jackie.''

''Do you care about the rest of the crew the same way?''

''Yes,'' she said firmly, and then, ''I think so. They haven't put me to the test. He didn't want to miss work, Sage. He didn't *want* to be late. He would apologize and explain, and all the while you knew he'd embarrassed himself again, dug a deeper hole for himself. And when he was doing well, he was such a good worker, and so willing—''

''Megan.'' He touched her shoulder and waited until she looked into his eyes. ''A man can drown in pity, and you're pouring it out by the bucketful.''

She stared for a moment. ''Is that what it is? Pity?''

''It sure sounds like it. Can you tell me you respected Jackie? One rational, independent adult to another—did you think of him that way?'' She looked down at her hands and gave her head a quick shake. ''You felt sorry for him.''

She lifted her eyes to his, and they were swimming. ''I didn't mean to drown anyone. I got close enough to see his boot, lying there in the grass.'' She closed her eyes, and her throat grew painfully raspy. ''The color of his shirt—I saw that, too. I feel bad about Jackie's death, Sage. I really do.''

''Grief is okay,'' he said gently, and he slid his arm behind her neck and squeezed her shoulder. She tipped her head to the side, resting her forehead on his arm. "It's honest and natural. And what I see in you now...is grief."

Chapter 8

This is where we've got problems." Sage pointed to the map on Megan's desk. "This is pretty soft stuff."

"The old roadbed has a quarter mile of washboard there," Megan said as she looked down his arm at the spot he was indicating. "The culvert should go in here."

"Yeah, but the hill's there. I'm working down here, and that clay just doesn't quit."

"Maybe one culvert won't do it," she decided as she opened a plastic sandwich bag. "How far down are you?"

"I've scraped off a couple of feet. You're going to end up with a real dip if you don't make some adjustments there."

"I need to get down there this afternoon. Now..." She examined the sandwich, wondering what chance there was that her cooler had transformed it into something interesting since she'd put it together that morning. "I'll trade you half a tuna sandwich for almost anything else."

He pushed the map aside and leaned his hip against the desk. "How about canned chopped meat?" he offered. She looked doubtful. "Liverwurst? What about tongue?" Even as his eyes danced, he wondered what he thought he was doing, teasing her. He knew he'd allowed too much friendliness to seep into this relationship, but he couldn't seem to resist.

"Which is it?" she asked, her eyes warming to his.

"Which would you like?"

They let the question stand between them for a moment before he reached across the desk and dragged his black lunchbox closer. He produced a plastic-wrapped sandwich and handed it to her. "Corned beef on rye. Be my guest."

"Just half." She tried to exchange half of hers for it, but he shook his head.

"I hate tuna."

"I can't let you go hungry." She pushed his sandwich back at him.

He edged away as it occurred to him that there were all kinds of hunger. "I've got another one." He proved it to her, then nodded at her cooler. "If you've got anything cold to drink in there, I'll trade for a share of that. All I've got is hot coffee."

"On a day like this?" She hiked herself up to sit on the desk, flipped back the lid of her cooler and brought out a bottle of lemon-flavored mineral water. "I've got another one."

Sage watched her unscrew the cap on the bottle before she handed it to him. They'd just discussed a hitch in the project like two professional equals, and now she was opening a bottle of water for him and worrying about whether he was going to get enough to eat. In recent weeks he'd become comfortable with their working relationship. If the crew had been taking bets on anything when he went into the office the way they had when Taylor had been working with her, Sage figured they'd given it up. Heads no longer turned at the sight of the two of them together, and he believed they were now seen as a team. Engineer and construction foreman. But when they took a break, he wanted to tease her about little things like sandwiches, and he wanted to smile at her in a way that had nothing to do with the project they shared. He took the bottle from her hand, and his fingers brushed over hers. His eyes met hers, and he saw a woman.

The flavored water slid over his tongue like firefighter's foam. Thanks, he thought. I needed that. When he lowered the bottle and looked at her again, he trusted the tart bubbles to eradicate any longing his eyes might betray. He scowled at the bottle. "You actually *pay* for this stuff?"

"The first taste is always the worst," she assured him. "Once you get used to it, it's sort of like the champagne of bottled water."

"Champagne?" He studied the label before he tried it again. Swallowing, he nodded. "You'd have to acquire the taste for it, I guess."

She uncapped another bottle. "I especially enjoy this when the weather's hot. It quenches your thirst better than sweet, sticky pop."

He admired the delicate curve of her neck as she lifted her chin and tipped the bottle to her lips. There was no denying the heat. It might reach a hundred degrees before the day was out, he thought, but Megan wouldn't wilt. She would probably bloom, in fact, if the color in her cheeks was any indication. Her face glowed with a soft sheen. Nothing sticky, he thought, but maybe sweet. He imagined touching his lips to her forehead, then licking them. She wouldn't be salty. She would be smooth and sweet.

"I can't resist sweets," he said. She lowered the bottle and blotted her upper lip with the back of her hand. He smiled. "I'm worse than a kid."

"Mmm, but when it's this hot—" She took the sandwich he'd given her in both hands and studied it. "A cold beer would be good with this."

"Sure would." She gave him the surprised look of someone who'd just stepped on his toe. He laughed. "You'll get no argument from me on that point. I've always been a great fan of cold beer on hot days."

"A fan," she said quickly. "That's what we need in here. Better yet, a bathtub. I'd spend my lunch hour in it."

"Really? We'd have a hell of a time keeping the maps dry." He bit into his sandwich and decided that the drink was more appealing than the food was at this point. "Ever tried a sweat bath?"

"You mean, like a sauna?"

"Sort of." The sauna lacked the spiritual quality of a sweat bath, but he doubted her interest in that aspect. "It's better than an ordinary bath. You sweat. You get rid of all the excesses and the need to indulge in excesses. You cleanse yourself from the inside out, and *then* you take a cool bath."

"Is this something *you* do? Like a religious thing?"

"Like a religious thing." It was probably her use of the word *thing* that made him hold back. He found himself teasing rather than sharing. "A tribute to Grandmother, sort of like buying her flowers or something."

"How often do you do this?"

"As often as I need to." He lifted an eyebrow. "How often do you bathe?"

She ignored the question, suddenly intrigued. "Do you do this as a group?"

"Not usually. Not unless—"

"I mean as part of the Medicine Wheel program." She'd conjured up a picture of him and Regina, and the jealousy was back. He studied her for a moment, taking the time to make her uncomfortable. Damn him—he was reading her mind!

"Men and women don't sweat together. At least, not in the sweat lodge."

She squirmed on the desktop. "You just..." She drew the idea of separation in the air. "The men in one, and the women..."

"I usually do it on my own or with a medicine man. It's a personal experience, not a party." She didn't understand, but something in the way she looked at him told him that she wanted to. "It isn't like a health club, Megan. It's more like—"

"Like going to church?"

"Well, no, not exactly." It occurred to him that it wasn't like anything else, which was probably why he did it.

"More like yoga?" she persisted.

"I don't know what yoga's like." He laughed. "It's like a sweat bath. Maybe sometime you'll, uh . . ."

"I'd like to." It seemed incredible, but she was suddenly anxious to experience heat even more intense than that inside the trailer. "How hot does it get? You don't think I'd faint, do you?"

"Not you. I think you'd come through with flying colors once you understood what it was all about."

"I'll have to read up on it. You know, you've given me lots of food for thought, Sage. Things I want to know more about."

He laughed. "I'm not even going to ask what."

"Well, things." She worked on her sandwich for a moment before she added, "I like to read up on topics that catch my interest. I've got a lot of time at night for reading. Not much to do in Hot Springs."

"There's that big natural springs swimming pool," he suggested, suddenly feeling uncomfortable.

She shrugged. "Yeah, that's kinda fun." She followed the sandwich with an apple, which she offered to share, but Sage declined with a shake of his head. "I've read a lot about Native American history, but not much on religion. What would you recommend?"

In addition to a reading list, he could have suggested a movie. He could have suggested they see it together. He climbed into the seat of the big yellow earth mover and brought it to life with the flick of a key. The thought had crossed his mind many times, but he'd dismissed it as a crazy notion. He didn't know how to socialize.

His wife had wanted what her people called a "social life," and he'd never really understood what that was. Whatever it was, it always involved drinking, and when he got drunk, she always accused him of ruining their social life. He'd thought he'd been doing what he was supposed to do. Hell, he'd always been the life of the party. Nobody ever made much of an impression on him when they were "socializing," at least not that he remembered. The people and their relationships and his relationship to them all ran together in a hazy blur.

Now he went to Medicine Wheel, and he worked. He had friends in both places. Relationships were clear to him. On the job there were fellow workers. In Medicine Wheel there were people who cared about his recovery as much as he cared about theirs. But this idea of a social life was still vague. He wondered if there was a sober way to manage it. What would it be like to be with a woman and be stone cold sober? Why did the words "stone" and "cold" seem to slip in front of "sober" so automatically? The cold part scared him. He'd given it a try a couple of times when he'd first sobered up, and cold was the only way he could describe it.

Megan was different. He thought about her in a way he remembered thinking of no one else. It wasn't in terms of his own needs. He liked to remember the talks they had about roadbeds and ranching, about solving problems with ground water and saving the bald eagle. He was haunted by the trickle of perspiration he'd seen slip down her temple, and he imagined brushing it away. Nothing more. Just to be granted the privilege of touching her face without asking, without explaining.

He wanted to be close to her, and the thought was frightening. She kept coming into his life through different doors, and he knew now that he wanted her to keep coming back. He wanted her to open his private doors, but he wanted her to understand what she was getting into. He wanted her to put away her blinders and still be able to accept him. Hell, he wanted her to be able to *like* him. That, in a nutshell, was his fear. Maybe without all the bravado, there was really nothing about him for a woman to like.

Her pickup was still parked beside the trailer. She'd spent part of the afternoon looking over the portion of the roadbed about which Sage had expressed concern, and he'd half hoped she would have left for the day. They'd been back to being engineer and foreman, and there hadn't been any problems. A problem with the contour of the grade, maybe, but no problem with the engineer and the foreman. After she'd left the site, he'd started working himself into a lather about talking to her again, this time about Megan and Sage. The notion wouldn't go away, so he decided to drive back to the office and satisfy himself that she was no longer there. So much for being taken off the hook.

"Hey, you're still here?" He pulled the door shut with a sweaty palm.

Megan looked up from her calculations and smiled—casually, she hoped. She'd seen him drive up. She'd put the pencil down then, but she was holding it again for effect. "I'm just about finished. I'm surprised *you're* still here."

He sat on the edge of the desk and twisted his head to get a look at her figures. They all ran together. His mouth was dry. "You got it all solved now?"

"I think so. I think we pretty much worked it out this afternoon. A little more elevation and another culvert." He nodded, and she tossed her pencil on top of her figures. "Is the roof finished yet?"

"The roof?" She disappeared behind the desk and came back up with her lunch cooler. "Uh, well, the sheathing, yeah. That's done." He checked his watch. "I'm on my own time now, right?"

She moved around the desk, feeling the heat from his eyes. She smiled. "If you say so. You're the fore-man."

"Yeah, well...what I want to bring up is strictly personal business, so, uh, just so you know..."

"Nothing you say at this point will be used against you." She braced both hands on top of her cooler and leaned toward him. "What's on your mind?"

"Tell you the truth, it's you."

"Me?" she asked innocently.

"Yeah, you." He sprang away from the desk and shoved his hands into his pockets. "Don't act like you're surprised, Megan. You've been on my mind a lot lately."

"We've been around each other a lot lately."

"Yeah, I know. You have a way of appearing out of the woodwork." He lowered his voice and admitted, "Even when you're not really there."

"Am I giving you nightmares?"

He turned and caught her whimsical smile. "I might as well tell you that you'd be crazy to go out with me."

"Would I?"

"Yeah, you would. I don't know the first thing about dating." He turned to the window and stared at the tool box in the back of his pickup. "It seems like I went from pulling girls' braids in school to pulling them down on the backseat of a car after a rodeo and a six pack. There weren't any dates."

"Then how did you get to know your wife?"

"I didn't. And I never let her get to know me." He faced her and leaned back against the windowsill. "Somewhere along the line I just laid claim to her, I guess. I used to rodeo a lot, and she'd come along. When she got pregnant, we figured it might be nice to get married." He gave a mirthless chuckle as he shook his head. "It wasn't nice. Neither one of us was any good at it. After a while it seemed like all I did was argue with her or screw her." He saw her eyes widen, and he felt a little sick. He glanced away. "There's no other word for it," he said quietly. "That's all it was."

"I don't understand why you're telling me all this."

He sighed heavily. "Because at this point in my life, I'm about as backward as they come. I ought to be telling you that I've just had bad luck with women, because I know that would stir up those caretaking instincts of yours right now. But the truth is, women haven't had much luck with *me*."

"Your life has changed a great deal since...since you were married."

"Yeah, I know." He studied the toe of his boot. "That's why I was thinking...maybe if I went slow..."

She waited. The seconds ticked by, and she held her breath. When he looked up at her, she saw the hope in his eyes. "Are you asking me out, Sage?"

He gave a crooked smile. "Trying to."

She smiled back. "Then you really shouldn't tell me all your faults first."

"You mean I'm not going about this right?"

It was something she knew she said often. Laughing, she shook her head sympathetically. "About as backward as they come."

"That's the way I felt when we had lunch together today." He straightened away from the window and approached her slowly. "I figured we had a nice friendship going, and it was probably all wrong for us to start sweating over each other's hungry looks." He saw the color rise in her cheeks, but she didn't back away. He took another step. "I don't wanna mess things up between us, Megan."

"Then let's keep it simple," she suggested. "How about a movie?"

He smiled at the idea of keeping it simple. That had been a survival tactic of his for the last four years.

"You said you like horses," he reminded her. "I'd like to take you for a ride up in the Badlands, out by my place."

"I'd like that, too," she told him.

Chapter 9

It had been agreed that Megan would pack a picnic lunch and Sage would provide the beverages and transportation to the Badlands. She wasn't one to fuss over food, especially in her little motel kitchenette, but she took extra care with this meal. She knew they were both tired of sandwiches.

Sage had been waiting for her. He hailed her from the corral when she slowed her pickup near the trailer. When she pulled up near the barn, he hopped down from the railing and walked over to the truck, shutting the door for her after she'd emerged with her cooler.

"Ready to ride?" he asked as he made an obvious point of appraising her attire. She wore a yellow knit tank top, jeans and a pair of cowboy boots that had been sitting in her closet for years. "You'll be getting a good dose of sun today," he warned.

"That's exactly what I want." He looked good in his straw cowboy hat. The wheat color contrasted sharply with his black hair and brown skin, and the loose weave of the brim created a pattern of sunlight and shadow over his face. He wore a blue chambray shirt with the sleeves rolled nearly to his elbows, and his jeans fitted his long legs and slim hips as though they'd been tailored for him.

He ushered her through the narrow corral gate. "When you said you liked horses, I guess I assumed you had some experience with them."

"I do, but I haven't done any riding since I was in college."

"I'm going to put you on the sorrel so you won't have to contend with mama's baby." He nodded toward the colt. "If she thinks he's having trouble keeping up, she might get broncky."

"Broncky?"

"She'll start balking. She might even offer to crow-hop a little, like a bronc. That sorrel is a nice trail horse, though. I use him all the time. I've also got two young mares out in the pasture." He gestured toward the hills. "They're only green broke."

Megan saw that the horses were saddled. She held the cooler up for Sage's consideration. "What'll we do with this?"

"Transfer it to the saddlebags." He took the cooler over to the sorrel's side and began arranging its contents in one of the pouches of a set of canvas saddlebags, which was already strapped behind the cantle of the saddle. "You've got plenty of plastic ice in here. I'll put some on the other side, with the drinks."

"I hope you like fried chicken." She examined the construction of the bag while he added ice on the other side. "Do you think it'll be okay in here?"

"If you fried it, I think it's past complaining." She saw his grin above the horse's rump. "I'm not going to let it sit in there too long. It smells great. Need any help getting up?"

"Oh, no, thanks. I'm a cowboy, too." But she found that the stirrups had already been shortened for her, and the sorrel stood taller than she'd realized. She soon had her leg twisted up like one of the chicken wings she'd fried, with only the tip of her toe in the stirrup. She was grasping for any leather within reach when she heard him move in close behind her, chuckling.

"A short one," he allowed as he put his hands at her waist. "And quite a contortionist. Just let me give you a little boost, cowboy."

His strength took her by surprise. She was high in the air before she knew it. Reaching for the saddle horn became an afterthought as she swung her leg over the horse's back. "Thank you," she managed as she straightened in the saddle.

"Anytime." He led the mare through the gate. The colt pranced behind, apparently anxious for an outing. Sage closed the gate behind Megan, and she watched the fluid ease with which he swung himself into the saddle.

"It's only because your legs are longer," she muttered.

He flashed her a smile. "Eat your corn flakes, cowboy. You might stretch a little."

They rode through three quarter sections of pasture that were dotted with cows and calves before Megan turned in the saddle to tell him, "I've seen more than fourteen cows out here."

"Really?" He scanned the grassy flat. "They must be reproducing faster than I thought. How many do you think are out here?"

"Well, I'd say at least—" She frowned and peered past her shoulder at his deadpan expression. "I'd say you know exactly."

"Exactly a hundred and ninety-four," he told her with a smile. "I'm pasturing cattle for another rancher. Pays my lease and some of my other expenses."

"I thought this was your land."

"Not all of it," he told her. "Some of it belongs to other members of the family, and I lease it from them through the BIA. I also have a grazing permit for some park land."

"Why doesn't the other rancher just lease the land himself?"

"This is one of the few instances in which there's a legal advantage to being an Indian. White ranchers can only get the lease if no Indian wants it. I've got the lease, and he pays me to pasture his stock."

She peered ahead at the wall of wind- and water-worn rock that stretched across the horizon like an ancient, craggy ruin. The sheer rock face appeared to provide nothing that could sustain any life. "I don't see how you could keep any cattle up there," she said. "You don't, do you? Nothing could live up there."

"Wait till we get closer," he suggested. "The only way to see the Badlands is to ride through them."

"I've only driven *past* them," she said.

"Then you're in for an experience." He grinned at her. "You seem to have an interest in things that might be just a little on the bad side."

They rode into the Badlands. Once they passed the first grassy steps and their eroded risers, Megan felt as though she were being enveloped by draws lined with strange, striated tan and gray walls. Some of the eroded uprights supported grass-topped tables. Others were barren, carved by the wind to resemble the turrets and spires of gray and sandy-walled castles. Many of the walls were pockmarked with holes, as though they had been sprayed by a giant's machine gun. Sage explained that these were the burrows of a kind of bee, the solitary bee, whose larvae were hunted by pecking birds. Other rocky faces were visited by cliff swallows, who darted in and out of the clay blisters they'd fashioned on the sheer rock and tended their nests within.

"Some things live here." Sage pointed to the gray-green vegetation that dotted the landscape.

"Yucca," she acknowledged. "And lots of sage."

"Tough stuff."

They followed the lazy curve of a mud flat, which seemed a poor excuse for a creek bank, but then, the narrow stream of water seemed a poor excuse for a creek. The animals that had been there earlier in the morning obviously found cause to disagree. Sage pointed to crisscrossing lines of tracks, clearly embedded in the mud. "Coyote," he said. "Rabbit. Couple of pronghorns." He pointed at the ground ahead and said in the same even tone, "Sasquatch."

Megan twisted in her saddle, studying the tracks as she passed. "Sasquatch? You mean . . . ? Those look more like a horse's tracks."

"Sasquatch's horse. His big feet are killing him."

Once again she scowled at him. "Sasquatch my foot."

"Yours are too small." He scowled back, then broke into another of his engaging grins.

"You're an awful tease, Parker."

"You're an easy mark, McBride." He reined his horse toward the hill. "Come on. There's a spot up here I want to show you."

They picked their way among the huge mushrooms of clay, undercut by the rushing water of spring storms, and climbed the puckers of rainwash toward a grassy upper level. They rode to the edge of the table, where Sage dismounted with the announcement, "Let's eat."

He helped her down and handed her the saddlebags before picketing the horses several yards away from one another to avoid any contentious kicking while they nibbled at the plentiful grass. The colt was free to romp, but like the toddler he was, he never strayed far from his mother. Megan was sorry she hadn't packed some sort of blanket, but Sage didn't seem to notice that anything was missing as he settled on the natural cushion of curly buffalo grass and broke out a bottle of mineral water and one of orange soda. She smiled when he offered her the lemon water, and his eyes danced back with the obvious satisfaction of having remembered her favorite flavor.

The wind exercised unusual restraint for this barren part of the world, giving them only a pleasant midday breeze. Content with one another's company, they shared the food without much conversation. When they were down to the last of their drinks, Sage pointed across the chasm toward a higher wall and a higher grassy table. "That's where my grandfather's scaffold stood. That's the spot I wanted to show you."

"I thought scaffold burials were illegal," Megan said as she gazed at the high flat that seemed to have a special place in the sun.

"They are. But my grandfather said that beyond death the law meant nothing. He told my mother that his spirit wouldn't rest unless his body went to the scaffold in the old way. She chose to defy the law rather than her father's dying wish."

"How old was he when he died?"

"Ninety-four. He died in the cabin—the one I was born in." He plucked a single blade of grass and stuck the end in his mouth as he watched the grass across the way ripple in the sunshine. He imagined the scaffold standing above it. "I was only about six, but I remember hearing the death rattle in his throat. He crooned for days before he finally went. He spoke no English on his deathbed."

"Ninety-four! That's amazing."

Sage nodded, still gazing at the spot that brought back these memories. "He outlived his sons and all but his youngest daughter—my mother. He said it was because he shunned the 'white sins'—flour, sugar, salt and alcohol. My older brothers and sisters remember him better than I do, but I remember his death very well."

"It must have been terrible for you to watch him die."

"No, it wasn't. It was peaceful. He wasn't shut up in some antiseptic hospital with tubes stuck in his nose. Life went on as usual around him, and he was at peace when he slipped away from us." He leaned on one elbow and stretched his long legs out in the grass. "Then they prepared to raise him toward the sun. There was a lot of whispering and scurrying around to get it done quickly. I knew everyone was afraid the scaffold would be found, and I felt as though I had been entrusted with an important secret."

"Did the talk of restless spirits scare you?"

"Of course." He looked at her solemnly. "It's supposed to. People around here have a healthy respect for spirits. Most of my grandfather's personal possessions were buried with his bones after they were picked clean. The rest were given away."

Megan drew her knees up to her chin and wrapped her arms around them. "But surely you wanted to keep some things as remembrances."

"It might be safe to keep some things—things that weren't very personal."

"Safe?"

He looked into her eyes and tried to assess the degree to which she might have opened her mind during the time they'd spent together. Her gaze was clear and bright. Curious, yes, but her eyes didn't ridicule him as he had, at times, ridiculed himself for the old beliefs. He'd found that he could mock them, call them superstitions, brush them away with an impudent gesture and call himself a modern man, but the instinctive acceptance of them wouldn't leave him.

"They're called *wanagi*," he explained. "Spirits of the departed ones. I've told myself that when you live out here on the prairie, the night sounds alone are bound to make you believe in ghosts. When it comes right down to it, I can't explain them away to my own satisfaction. When I go hunting, I still leave a piece of my kill for the *wanagi*."

"Have you ever seen or heard anything yourself that convinced you of the presence of the spirits?" she asked. The mere idea was interesting, but the underlying thrill of fear was irresistible. Megan hugged her legs tighter.

He sat up and tossed aside the stem of grass he'd been chewing. "There was Jackie," he said quietly, feeling the risk in the pit of his stomach each time he said the dead man's name aloud.

"You mean, Jackie's ghost?"

"Something called me that day, Megan. I knew he was there, and I knew he'd been trying to tell me he was there." He watched her take the information and turn it over carefully in her mind. "Do you believe me?"

"Of course I believe you. I was there."

"Did you feel it, too? That weird tugging, that—"

"No. I just felt scared watching you. I knew it was going to be something terrible."

He leaned closer. "Do you believe it was Jackie's ghost?"

"I don't know." She glanced across the chasm again. "I guess I believe there are some things that aren't easy to explain. Maybe they don't have to be explained. Maybe they just *are*."

He smiled, satisfied. Just that much margin in her thinking was enough. He got to his feet, offering her a hand. "Let me take you to another place where things 'just are'. Might save you a trip to the library."

They rode through an eroded gully whose history was recorded in dark and light striations, which seemed to change color as her viewing angle changed. A hawk glided above them on an invisible current of hot air, and on a nearby plateau a prairie dog barked a warning to its burrowing community.

"As beautiful as this land is, I can't imagine it's worth leasing for cattle," Megan said. "There isn't much grass."

"There's more than meets the eye. And there's good shelter in these breaks. It doesn't support too many head, but the lease is pretty reasonable. Besides, I like to come here. I don't have to try too hard to imagine what it was like here a hundred, two hundred, years ago. It was just like this."

She tried to imagine what he would have looked like a hundred years ago, without the hat, without the boots or Western saddle. It wasn't difficult. His hooded eyes were crinkled at the corners, and his cheekbones were chiseled and high. The whole effect was to protect the eyes of a man who faced limitless sky, sun and wind every day of his life. Sage belonged to these stony, wind-worn hills as surely as his grandfather had.

They came to another stream and followed its winding path through a valley. The water was clear and inviting, and the sun overhead seemed to grow hotter by contrast. Megan saw the willow skeleton of a small dome off in the distance and felt her blood course a little faster as they approached it. He was about to show her something special. He was about to confide in her again.

They watered the horses before tethering them to either end of a fallen, sun-bleached cottonwood. Sage led Megan to the small willow dome. "This is covered with hides and blankets to make the sweat lodge," he explained. He walked around it, indicating the steps with his hands. "You build a fire and heat the rocks outside." She noted the supply of stones, waiting in a small mound. "You roll the hot rocks inside, pour water over them for steam and sweat like crazy. When you've had enough, you jump into the creek."

"What a shock that must be." She examined the way the slender, flexible willows were curved and lashed together. "You just sit there and sweat?" she asked.

"Well, you ... pray." He remembered when prayer had been suggested to Megan at Medicine Wheel; he'd had the sense that she'd rejected the idea as ineffective. He remembered a time when it had been suggested to him and he'd laughed, too.

"What do you pray for?" When she heard the question, she glanced up quickly, recognizing her own audacity. "I mean, generally speaking. I don't mean to pry or anything. I just wondered if there was a sort of..."

"Liturgy?" He smiled and shook his head. "I don't know of any. When you do this with a medicine man, he sings in Lakota. Unfortunately, I don't speak much Lakota. So I just pray."

He ran his hand along the smooth curve of a willow rib. It occurred to him that this woman was important to him, and it made him a little nervous to speak of these things to her. It seemed more natural to tease her, to flash his smile and put them both at ease. But he wanted something else this time. It somehow seemed right to talk with her.

"I'm looking for healing, Megan. I'm trying to put the pieces back together, and I'm finding out that the pieces of me go way back. There's a spiritual connection that got severed somewhere along the way."

"But so much time has passed, and so much has changed."

"Some things have changed. I used to think they were major changes—the way we get our food and clothing, the kind of homes we have. But our basic needs haven't changed. We still eat. We still put clothes on our bodies and live together in some kind of shelter. The missionaries and the government denied us our ceremonies, and we've always been a very spiritual people. We tried to make do or do without. Everything got watered down and wrung out. Pretty soon we were left with the desiccated remains of what we'd once been. We imitated ourselves for tourists, and we looked for something to kill the pain, something to fill the void. Alcohol seemed to be a ready cure for all that ailed us."

He squatted beside the mound of stones, resting one knee on the cracked hardpan. "I pray for healing," he told her as he lifted a fist-size stone and weighed it in his hand. "I pray for the strength to put my self-indulgence aside so I can hold my head up in the community. I pray for wisdom. Generation after generation has been stripped layer by layer. Some things are gone for good. We need to replenish ourselves. I want to know how."

"You need jobs," Megan said as she stood close and watched him. "In this day and age, in order to get the food, the clothing and the shelter, you have to have a job."

"Sure." He looked up, smiled and got to his feet, bouncing the rock in his palm. "We need to support ourselves. The government payoffs can't begin to redeem us. We need to look within ourselves, which is a tough place to start. Most of us are scared to death we'll find there's nothing there."

"Nothing there! That's ridiculous, Sage. Look how far you've come."

He stared at her for a moment, giving her a sense, as he had at other times, that he was looking through her at the workings of her brain. He turned from her suddenly and mounted an assault on a sloping embankment.

"Sage?" She hurried after him to the top of the slope, which was lush with needle-and-thread grass. "What did I say? How can you feel—"

He spun on his heel. "I can feel whatever I feel. Don't tell me to deny it. If I level with you about a real, deep and abiding fear, don't tell me it's ridiculous. Don't try to pat me on the head and say, 'You've come a long way, baby.' And, by God, don't you try to tell me you never in your life doubted yourself, Miss Megan, highway engineer.''

"Well, of course, I've—"

"Of course! Of course! Is it really that black and white? Is everything really that clear to you? My God, you must sleep well at night."

She hated herself for lowering her gaze, but his emotion had filled his own eyes with such power that she couldn't bear the pressure any longer. "I only meant to say that *I* see a lot in you," she said quietly. "Talent, ambition, determination..."

"And I told you that I pray for healing, wisdom and the strength to face another day. What you see isn't enough. Don't belittle my needs or my fears.... Don't..." Her eyes were too round and blue and filled with regret. He lifted his hand and placed it gently along her jaw, tracing the sharp curve below her ear with his long middle finger. He knew he could drown in those eyes. He rubbed her chin with his thumb, and the order became a soft plea. "Don't."

She stood there looking up at him, her stomach fluttering. "Don't what?"

"Don't look at me like that."

"I'm confused, Sage. I seem to say all the wrong things, and I don't want to."

"I know." He wanted to kiss her. God, he wanted to kiss her!

"I only meant to say that I believe in you."

His smile was tentative. "I'm a poor excuse for something to believe in, Megan. I'm still trying to understand what *I* believe in." He slid his hand the length of her arm and took her by the hand. "You've heard of *hanble ceya*, the vision quest?"

She nodded as he pulled her down to sit with him on the ground. "Don't you see some kind of an animal or something after you starve yourself for several days?"

He looked at the clouds overhead as he chuckled. "Yeah, right. Fast for three days so you can hallucinate herds of buffalo and skies full of eagles."

"That's what happened in *A Man Called Horse*," she reminded him. What did she know other than what she'd read, or seen in the movies?

He tapped his forefinger on her knee. "A man called Sage is here to tell you that there's a lot more to it."

"You've done it?"

He nodded. "Lakota tradition teaches that there are several aspects of the human soul. There's the part that lives on in the afterlife. There's also the shade— you know, the ghosts we talked about that haunt the living if they're not respectful. There's the earthly soul. That's the best part of you—your talents, your life's purpose, your ability to be noble and give love. It's that part of the soul that the vision quest is directed to. *Hanble ceya* is crying for a vision of your world and your place in it."

"Did you have a vision?"

He thought for a moment as he looked down at the crusty mud of the creek bank and the frame of his sweat lodge. By the very act of bringing her to this place he had made a decision to share himself with her. It wasn't necessary that she believe as he did, only that she respect what he believed. If he answered her question, he knew he would have to take the risk of being scoffed at in the hope of securing acceptance.

"I went to the hill three times." He smiled and shook his head as he recalled three fasts, three sweats, three days alone in the vision pit on each of three occasions. "I must have been a really hard case for the spirits to crack. The third time they saw me coming, they took pity on me and gave me a vision."

It was a confidence. She knew she had no right to ask for more, but she seemed unable to contain her interest. "I don't suppose you can talk about...about your vision."

He raised his brow. "I'll tell you this much: it had me building a road. And there was a wheel." He leaned back to allow his hand access to his front pocket, from which he pulled a two-inch ring with four spokes all covered with red, white, yellow and black quillwork. He handed it to her, saying, "It's a medicine wheel. I took it as my symbol and wore it when I did the Sun Dance."

"The Sun Dance!" Her eyes widened. "With all that torture and suffering?" Maybe she was thinking Hollywood again. "Or is it more ritualistic nowadays?"

"You mean, is it all just a show?" She returned his medicine wheel, and he held it between his finger and thumb, considering. "Generally, outsiders aren't allowed to watch, but tradition says there must be witnesses, those who will care for the dancers, attest to the fact that the pain was endured and learn from what they see." He lifted his eyes to hers. "Wasn't it so with the crucifixion? Without witnesses, no one would know. It would be as though nothing happened."

He reached out to pluck a blade of grass as he continued. "We've crippled ourselves by perfecting this 'secret suffering,' this 'stiff upper lip.' I spent a lot of time trying to avoid pain, numb it, deny it altogether. Others may know about the pain because they've heard gossip, but they mind their own business, because they're embarrassed by it."

She remembered his admission of pain at the loss of his children before the Tribal Council. Yes, she'd been embarrassed by it. "I would be afraid to suffer like that in public," she confessed. "I'd make a fool of myself."

"We need to admit the pain before we start healing. Through the Sun Dance, I accepted pain as part of life, and I made it a spiritual offering." He leaned to one side and pocketed his amulet. "That was my way. It may not make sense to you."

"It does," she said quickly. "It makes a great deal of sense. It just seems like such a...drastic measure."

"It *is* a drastic measure," he explained. "It's often done when someone in the family is very ill, or, in the old days, when you'd had a close call in battle and you knew damn well it could have gone either way. You're still scared. I had a close call and—" He looked directly into her eyes, and his voice barely rose above the rustle of the wind in the tall grass "—sometimes I'm still scared."

"Like...when you saw Jackie?"

"Yeah." His eyes glazed with the memory. "When I saw my own face lying in the grass and felt a piece of him in me."

"Does it help?" she asked. "Are you stronger, having done the dance?"

"I believe I am."

"Were you pierced? Where..."

She watched with fascination as he began unbuttoning his shirt. When he reached his belt, he pulled the fabric free of his pants and flicked the last two buttons open. He drew his shirt back to expose the scars—two puckered marks over his pectoral muscles. She wondered why she hadn't noticed them before. Identical and evenly placed, they were scars made by design, not by accident. He had borne them willingly in the hope of transcending the pain they caused.

Megan rose up on her knees as she lifted her hands to his chest, placing her fingertips over the scars. His skin was hot, and the small cords of scar tissue felt hotter still. He covered her hands with his and flattened them hard against his skin. She heard the catch in the deep breath he drew as he hooked the heels of his hands beneath her chin and curved his long fingers around her head. She looked up and saw the heat of his kiss in his eyes before she lifted her chin and accepted the offering hungrily with her mouth. Their kiss came tentatively in a quick coupling of moist lips. It came again and lingered longer, mouths moving over one another, exploring possibilities. It came a third time with mutual insistence, hard pressure, a soft whimper, a needy groan. Sage slid his arms around

Megan's shoulders and lay back in the grass, pulling her down with him.

His scars seared her palms. She caressed them with circular motions and kissed the lips that moved anxiously against hers. His belt buckle pressed against her stomach, and his manhood grew quickly between her thighs. The sudden intimacy at once frightened and thrilled her, swishing a peppery feeling up and down her thighs. Then he rolled with her, tucked her underneath him and invaded her mouth with his softly stroking tongue.

The heat of the sun diffused over his back and in his hair as he gloried in the way her hands felt against his skin. He made a conscious effort to transfer the sun's warmth into his kiss, to return the feeling of power she'd given him with just the touch of her hands. His body surged with it. His heart pounded with it. His soul was nourished with it.

"Megan, Megan, sweet Megan," he chanted near her ear. He pressed his cheek against her breast and hugged her close. "God, you make me feel good."

She smoothed the thick, damp hair over the back of his neck. "I don't think we need any hot rocks to work up a sweat, Sage."

He shook with silent laughter. "Out of the mouths of aroused women..." He lifted his head and offered one bitter-sweet kiss before sliding down to pull off her boot.

"Wha—"

He had them both off before she had time to protest further. "Socks, too," he ordered as he crooked his leg to work on his own boot.

She wasn't sure why she complied as he shed his shirt. When he grabbed her by the hand and pulled her to her feet, she caught the direction of his intentions. "No way!" Digging her heels in was difficult. Resisting his strength was impossible. "Sage!"

He spared her feet by sweeping her up in his arms and covering the ground easily; his own feet were accustomed to being bared on this creek bank. "It's mandatory, Megan."

"It is not! Not for me!" But she didn't fight him. She wouldn't mind wading in the little creek.

"After the sweat comes the—" Splash!

Megan bobbed to the surface and sputtered into his face. "What is this? The Indian Ocean?"

He laughed as he treaded water. "It cuts a deep channel here. You can swim, can't you?"

"You'd better hope I can!"

She could. After they'd traded splashes and displayed their best strokes, they emerged, laughing and dripping and shaking their fingers at one another in teasing admonition.

Megan pushed her short hair back from her face. "Now look!" she demanded, spreading her arms wide.

"I'm looking." He raised an appreciative eyebrow. "You sure are wet."

Her thin bra and summer top did little to hide the response of her nipples to the breeze's caress. She folded her arms across her chest. "At least you still have a dry shirt, Mr. Parker, and if you were any kind of gentleman, you wouldn't stand there drooling."

"I'm not drooling, I'm dripping, and you're the one who told me to look. I thought you were showing off." He grinned as he tossed his hair back. "I don't blame you, either. You look great." But he offered her his shirt, and when she reached for it, he openly admired the way her own shirt clung and her nipples beaded. "Who thought up the rules for being a gentleman, anyway?"

"Probably Queen Victoria." She made a spinning motion with her finger, and he turned away.

"No wonder I never made the grade."

While Megan peeled off all wet cloth above her waist and slipped into his shirt, Sage took a seat on the low bluff above the creek and hardly peeked. She tied the shirt under her bust to keep her jeans from getting it wet, then she joined him, letting her legs dangle over the edge of the grassy table, just as he did.

"I've never seen the Badlands the way you've shown them to me today," she told him. She gestured toward the striated sandstone wall across the creek. "It's like a huge sand paintng—the kind tourists buy in those plastic containers, all filled with layers of colored sand. One minute you think the wind and runoff have eroded all the life out of it." She leaned over to pluck a daisylike purple coneflower from a cluster rising in the tall grass. "The next, you come to a lovely spot like this."

"You would have ridden right by a spot like this," he said. "You have to get down and take a closer look. Here." He held up a sprig of white-striped greenery. "You know what this is?"

"Indian paintbrush."

"Shall I color you beautiful?" His eyes were made warm by his soft smile as he feathered the tuft over her cheek. " 'Behold, my brothers, the spring has come. The earth has received the embraces of the sun, and we shall soon see the results of that love.' "

She felt dewy inside. "That's wonderful. Is it yours?"

"If I said it was, would you believe me?"

"Of course."

He shook his head, still smiling, and put the Indian paintbrush in her hand. "You're an easy mark, Megan McBride. That was Sitting Bull."

"It sounds like something from the Old Testament."

"Then why were you ready to believe it was mine?"

"Because..." She glanced back down at the bright water flowing past them. "Because when you talk about the things that matter to you—your beliefs, your grandfather, Medicine Wheel—everything you say sounds...profound to me." She turned to him earnestly. "I don't care what you say, Sage. I think it's amazing what you've done, first for yourself and then for the others."

He wanted to bask in her praise. It felt so good to hear her say such things that he was tempted to allow her to romanticize his recovery. Hell, he might like being somebody's hero for a change. He knew he'd had enough of being the villain.

He straightened the collar of his shirt and lingered to touch the soft down on the back of her neck. "I wanted to make love to you. You know that, don't you?"

She nodded. "Wanting is natural. You didn't push."

"I don't have much experience with getting to be friends first. I want your friendship. I want to give you mine, for whatever it's worth."

"It's worth—"

"Kissing for?" He hooked his elbow behind her neck and brought her close enough to make the discovery that their friendship was indeed worth kissing for.

Chapter 10

Sage chewed on a toothpick and counted the shades of brown in the speckled linoleum floor of the Red Calf Community Center. There were fifteen people in the circle, and they were enjoying a time of reflection. To an observer, it might have seemed like a time of silence, but it wasn't. The voices of four children, who were chasing one another from corner to corner on the far side of the room, filled the people's ears. The consideration of what had been said thus far during the meeting filled their minds. The scent of the burning sweet grass that had been carried around the perimeter of the circle at the beginning of the meeting tantalized their nostrils. A steady rain pattered on the roof. The people moved easily from talk to no-talk and back to talk again, but no one felt compelled to fill the air with chatter.

Sage's reflections turned often to Megan and the day they'd spent together in the Badlands. He had wondered whether their working relationship would become awkward once they'd shared kisses. It hadn't. Monday morning had brought business as usual. Megan had gone to Pierre on Tuesday, and had stayed there for three days. He'd found himself missing her.

Initially it had come as a surprise. He'd allowed himself to miss Brenda and Tommy, but otherwise he'd generalized his loneliness. He missed women, family, even old buddies, but no one in particular other than the children. He was learning about real friendship through Medicine Wheel. Still, he spent most of his hours alone. Women, family and old buddies were difficult to deal with, so he'd put them all on the back burner in his daily life. Now he faced a longing to be with one person, one particular woman, and it scared him. He wanted too much too suddenly. He'd made too many mistakes in the past, and he didn't want to repeat them.

He knew all the wrong ways to treat a relationship, and he wasn't at all sure about the right ones. If a man weren't possessive, would a woman stick with him of her own accord? If he weren't jealous, would she still be faithful to him? If he weren't demanding, would she be inclined to give? And if he weren't any of those things, what would he be? Would he appear weak? Unmanly? He knew how to attract her, but when she started admiring him, what he was inside, not what he looked like outside, he had the feeling he was on shaky ground. Beneath the surface was a man who was learning to walk all over again, taking one careful step at a time. His experience had taught him how to build up the "masculine" image and take refuge behind it. His newly developing inclinations told him to try a little trust.

"We can't trust Floyd Taylor."

Sage straightened in his chair as he folded his arms over his chest and tuned his thoughts to Regina. No one stared at the speaker, but the circle assumed an attitude of listening.

"He's saying he's willing to take a temporary license," Regina continued. "He says he wants a chance to prove himself. That's what he's saying to the council, anyway. Out of the other side of his mouth, he's calling in a lot of old debts. He's saying no more credit at the store. People are getting scared."

"It's crazy to borrow money from him," old Bessie War Shirt grumbled. "You never know how he figures the interest."

"Don't ask him to explain it, either," another woman advised. "All you'll get out of it is that you owe him more money than you've got."

"We got no bank." Marvin Bad Heart was a new member who wasn't convinced that conditions could change. His voice was as expressionless as his face. "If we put Taylor out of business, we got no money. We've always borrowed money from the storekeeper. That's the way it's always been."

"We're gonna try it a different way," Sage said. "We can't be any worse off than we are now."

"Maybe," Marvin allowed. "But at least now we know what we got. May not be much, but we know what it is."

"I got a little insurance money," Regina announced quietly. "I think he'd want me to use it to open a store. He told me I was crazy to try it, but I think now...he'd like it if he could help me get it going."

The group allowed another quiet time to pass. They knew that Regina was wise not to mention her dead husband's name, but they felt his presence. They had a sense that Jackie approved of Regina's plan. Before the group broke up, there was more talk of support for Regina's store. Members also offered to help her prepare during the coming year for the giveaway that would commemorate the first anniversary of Jackie's death. The gifts to be given to his friends, especially those who had helped with the funeral, would be gathered over the course of the year. Regina would need help, particularly with the quilting.

Sage stood in the doorway and watched the other vehicles pull away from the building one by one. The slanting rainfall glittered just beyond their headlights. He thought of the low spot in the roadbed that was undoubtedly filling up with water. He could haul a compressor down there, get a pump going and maybe save the project some time and money. The yard light illuminated the moat that was fast gathering around the community center. Poor drainage, Sage thought. In this country, there was never enough water except when there was too much.

He paid no attention to the water running behind his back until it stopped. "Need any help?" he asked without turning around.

"The coffee pot's clean, and the windows are all closed." Regina closed a cupboard door. "My sister is watching the kids. We have time to talk if you want."

He turned now, smiling. "Aren't you all talked out?"

"You're not. You hardly said anything tonight." She leaned against the counter and waited, but he stayed where he was. His thoughts had strayed out into the night, and she thought it was a bad sign.

"I need to get going," he told her. "You ready?" He knew she wouldn't press. Megan would, but Regina wouldn't. She would let him keep his thoughts, if that was what he chose to do. But as he watched her shoulder her bag, he knew she was about to give him one of her own thoughts, anyway.

"You think it's a good idea, getting mixed up with another white woman?" Regina asked.

"Mixed up?" It surprised him to hear her use a term that was so direct and, for reasons that might surprise her, so appropriate. It made him laugh. He was mixed up, all right, but all on his own.

"We're trying to learn not to repeat our mistakes," Regina reminded him as she crossed the floor.

He let his smile fade, because she refused to return it. "I think of you as a sister, Regina. You know that."

"And I just lost one husband. I'm not looking for another one." Her boot heel skidded over the linoleum as she stopped beside him in the open doorway. "You're too important to this group. I don't want to see you getting your head messed up again by a white woman."

"My head was messed up before I ever met Riva. Our marriage was a disaster, but it wasn't because she was white.'

"She was no wife to you," Regina insisted.

"I was no husband to her." He dug his keys out of his pocket. "It was *my* head that was messed up." With the heel of his free hand he tapped his temple. "My *head*, not my heart. Somewhere along the line I must have put my heart in cold storage."

"No one in this group cares more than you do."

He lowered his hand slowly as he realized that he could think of no greater compliment. "I *have* changed, Regina." He looked at her hopefully. "I have, haven't I?"

His hard hat and slicker were no protection against the downpour. Once again he found himself kneeling in four inches of water and cussing at a pump. Nobody would have expected him to come back to the site after dark just to get a pump started. Rain was one of the inevitable impediments in road construction. If you dug a hole in a spot that held water and it rained, you lost time. Nobody came out in the middle of the night to rescue a roadbed.

But the changes Megan had made in her design had already increased costs. If this stretch washed out it would mean more time, which would mean more money. While Megan was in Pierre, this was Sage's baby. If the rain let up a little and the pump had a chance to catch up—hell, it was worth a try.

The rain and the compressor engine combined to drown out the sound of an approaching vehicle. Sage only knew it was there when he realized that another pair of headlights had joined his own. The extra light illuminated the problem—a tangled hose—and was welcome, at least on that score. But ever since someone had tampered with his pickup out here, Sage had been wary.

"Anything I can do to help?"

Megan's was the last voice he'd expected to hear. He squinted into the bright lights at the top of the rise. "You already did," he shouted. "I think we're all set. Got any coffee with you?"

"'Fraid not. I'll meet you back at the office."

The lights were burning in the trailer windows when he drove up. He leaped over the puddle at the foot of the steps and yanked the door open. He'd already abandoned his hat and slicker in the pickup, and he was drenched.

"Catch." A towel sailed across the room. Sage lifted his hand, and the towel flopped over this forearm like a horseshoe ringer.

He ruffled his hair with the towel, draped it around his neck and began unbuttoning his wet shirt. "When did you get back?"

"I got back to the motel a couple of hours ago."

Her hair was damp, but he could tell she'd just combed it. She wore a pink, V-neck cotton sweater and designer jeans, and her lips matched the sweater. Her feet were bare.

"My shoes got wet."

He moved his gaze back up to her face and realized that she'd watched him take inventory. She smiled, and he responded with a quizzical look. "What are you doing out here on a night like this? Didn't you think I'd take care of things?"

"I wouldn't have blamed you if you hadn't," she told him. "It's a lot to expect."

He phrased the question again. "What are you doing here?"

The tone of his voice said that he knew. He knew how restless she'd been, how she'd been wondering where he might be and what he might have on his mind. There had been a good chance she would find him here. They shared this much—this river of gravel becoming blacktop. There had been a good chance of meeting him on this common ground.

His scowl made her back away from the truth as she headed for the file cabinets. "I needed some figures from the daily reports."

"The hell you did." He tossed his shirt over a chair and moved in close behind her. She pulled out a file drawer, and he reached past her to stop it in its tracks. "Tell my why, Megan. Didn't you trust me to do the job?"

Her voice was small. "I knew you'd be here."

She let him push the drawer closed. He turned her toward him with a gentle hand, but cruel words came unbidden to his tongue. "Is this how it was with Karl Taylor? He backed you up against the files, and you—"

Her anger flashed in her eyes, but he braced his hands against the file cabinet, trapping her. "How can you even say that?" she whispered.

His chest tightened, and his brain did battle with itself. "I said it because... it was the first damn thing

that popped into my head. Walk away, Megan." He
dropped his hands to his sides, and his plea became
ragged. "Be smart. Walk away."

She stayed where she was, watching him struggle.
"Do you believe I led Karl on?"

"No," he admitted.

"Then why did you say that?"

"Old habits are hard to break." He couldn't stop
himself from touching her, from pulling her against
him and making it impossible for her to do as he'd
asked. "They're so damn hard to break." He lowered
his face into her hair and smelled the rain there.

"Maybe I can help," she whispered as she reached
around his back.

"Maybe I can make you miserable."

"Maybe," she whispered again. His smooth shoulder was there for her lips to touch. "If I'm willing to
let myself be miserable." She tipped her head back.
"Is that how you want it?"

He showed her how he wanted it. He pulled her tight
against his wet jeans and gave her a hard-driving kiss
that made her go all soft inside. One hand slid beneath her sweater and caressed her back, while the
other laid claim to her buttocks. His kisses made more
claims, and his tongue made promises. Megan spread
her hands over the corded muscles in his back as her
tongue welcomed his and her body strained with the
need to know more of him. When he lifted his head,
he realized she'd made claims, too. She'd taken his
breath away.

"I'm not miserable yet," she managed.

"I will be if we don't—" He pushed his fingers through her hair and shut his eyes as he tipped his forehead against her cool skin. "—go somewhere."

"My room's closest."

"My pickup's even closer." He cursed himself under his breath. Dragging her down on the seat of a pickup had been his first suggestion even when he knew damn well that that kind of a scene would be bad for both of them. "But we'd better take your room," he amended quickly. "And your truck. I'll leave mine, and we'll come back early."

She retrieved her shoes from behind the desk. Her slicker had gotten damp inside, and she shivered when she slipped it on. Sage grabbed his shirt and watched Megan fight with her shoes. They were wet and muddy, and her hands were unsteady.

"Come on, I'll carry you."

He was standing near the door with his shirt slung over his shoulder. She offered a tentative smile. "Is there a river out there I might get dropped in?"

He stuck his head outside, then ducked back in, smiling. "Wide as the Missouri. Come on," he urged as he cocked his head toward the open door.

She carried her shoes, holding them clear of his back as she was lifted into his arms. Sage sprinted through the puddles, and they laughed like mischievous children setting out for an adventure on a stormy night. He opened the door on the driver's side and put her in ahead of him, then got in behind her. She'd slid all the way over to the far side of the seat, and he wanted her closer. She read his message and scooted back, and he reached for her. Once he had her in his arms again, he kissed every drop of water from her face.

"God, I'm thirsty," he whispered. "Got anything to drink at your place?"

"If it's still raining when we get there, there'll be more water where that came from." She gave him a saucy smile. "I might be out of glasses."

He smiled back. "Maybe you'd like to take a shower."

It was only a ten-mile drive, but it seemed to take forever. Sage thought the whacking of the windshield wipers would drive him crazy. Megan watched the rain slash across the beams of light ahead.

"It's this one," she said, as though she'd just come awake.

Blue and yellow neon tubes made the words "Arrowhead Motel" jump out from the roadside. Then the U-shaped motor court came into view, with its zigzag of neon trim along the overhang.

The overdose of neon had never bothered Megan before. This was just a place to stay. But then, she'd never brought a man to her room before, and she suddenly wished the neon would evaporate. She wished her apartment weren't so far away. Sage had taken her to places that were part of him, and she was taking him to the Arrowhead Motel.

"Uh, Megan, do you think Kessler's would be open?"

They passed the motel, and she turned to him and stared. The drugstore?

Sage was suddenly aware of everything about himself that must have looked ridiculous. His pants were wet, his shirt was lying on the seat between them, he probably needed a haircut, since he could see a bunch of it hanging above his right eyebrow, and he had about thirteen dollars in his wallet and nothing else. *Nothing else.* It all came together in such an absurd package that he laughed aloud.

When had he last needed anything else? Thank God he had the thirteen dollars. It would have been embarrassing as hell to have to borrow money from her. It was going to be bad enough when he walked up to the cash register, looking like he'd just been let out of some cage, with that single purchase in his hand. If anyone tried to peek outside to get a look at who was with him, he would break their neck.

"What's so funny?" she asked.

He saw that she was just as uneasy as he was, and he tried to smooth things over with a smile. "I'm sorry. I know these things are supposed to be spontaneous." He lifted one shoulder to shrug away that expectation. "The guys with class are prepared to be spontaneous, right? The guys that order fancy wine and check out the cork." He saw the lights of Kessler's Drugstore. "I may be short on class, but I haven't run out of luck. It's still open. I need a candy bar or something. How about you?"

It felt good to laugh with him while he parked in a spot closer to the grocery store than the drugstore.

"Sage, it's raining. Look how far you have to walk."

She looked so damn cute, he had to kiss her. "Do I have to remind you that you've got your name emblazoned on the side of this pickup?"

"It says 'South Dakota Highway Department.'"

"Right." He planted another quick kiss on her mouth and grabbed his shirt. "Don't tell me what kind you like. Let me surprise you."

Megan slid down in the seat and grinned at the rain splattering the windshield. No one could accuse Sage Parker of being irresponsible. Megan McBride, maybe, but not Sage. Within minutes he was back with a small brown paper sack, from which he produced an almond-studded chocolate bar.

"Was I right?" He brushed the water off his forehead with his wet sleeve as he turned the pickup back onto the street.

"Excellent choice." She tore open the wrapper and took a bite. The creamy chocolate melted on her tongue. "Where's yours?"

He indicated the small bag next to his hip. "It's in there." He caught the movement of her hand. "Don't you dare," he warned. "Mine's for later."

"Have a bite of mine, then." She held it up to his mouth and heard him crunch into an almond.

Her room was neat. She could say that much for it. It held little more than a double bed and a bathroom. The kitchenette had a small stove and refrigerator, and the little Swedish modern table and two chairs did go with the blond headboard and the Eiffel Tower print that hung above it. Megan flicked the switch on a pole lamp that reached from floor to ceiling between the TV and a flat-cushioned arm chair.

"I don't know why they call this the 'Arrowhead Motel' when they have Paris on the wall." She kicked her shoes off quickly.

Sage heard the high note of nervousness in her voice. He closed the door behind him, then took off his muddy boots and set them near her shoes. The light was dim, but he stilled her hand before she turned another on. She glanced up at him, then at the room. "It's pretty dingy, isn't it?"

"You've seen where I live. At least you've got room to turn around."

"Your trailer is...quite masculine." He was still holding her hand, and it made her heart quicken.

He lifted one corner of his mouth in a half smile. "Is that a polite way of saying it's got no style?"

"No. It's a polite way of saying it's functional."

"So's this."

"But it's not pretty."

"You're pretty, Megan, and I swear to God, you're all I'm looking at right now." He hooked his arm behind her neck and leaned closer to whisper, "Are you scared?"

"I guess a little."

"We don't have to."

"I want to, Sage."

"Why?"

"Because I want to...share this with you."

He buried his lips in her hair, inhaled her scent and waited. She didn't turn his question back on him. What would he have said? Why did he want to do this? Because his blood coursed through him like river rapids, and if he didn't get inside her soon he was going to bust wide open? He wanted more reasons. Please make him capable of having one tender, unselfish reason somewhere in his mind. This woman was good to him, and he wanted to be good in return.

"I need a shower," he said hoarsely. "I've been down on my hands and knees in the mud, and that's not the way I want to come to you—not covered with mud."

"They have coin-operated machines here. I can wash your clothes for you while you—"

He shook his head. "I'll let you take care of me, just for tonight, but not that way."

"What way, then?"

"By sharing with me, just as you said." He tossed the bag on the bed and took her in his arms. "The best water I ever tasted came from your face, Megan." He dropped his voice close to her ear. "I need another drink."

"Sage..."

"Start by sharing a shower with me."

His kiss came hot and hard, but his clothes felt cold and soggy where he pressed himself against her. Her answer was to slide her hand between them and unbutton his shirt. She slipped her hand inside.

"You're cold," she whispered.

"Yeah." He nuzzled her neck. "Warm me."

She pushed his shirt off his shoulders, but she wouldn't let it go until it was draped over a chair. His wicked laughter sounded deep in his throat. "Megan, I don't care about my clothes. I care about yours." She stole a glance at him. "I want to undress you and touch every part of you while I do it. I want to do the things I never used to take the time for. And I'm not real sure..."

She laid her hands along his smooth cheeks. "We've waited a long time. Let's find out, Sage."

She raised her arms slowly, and he peeled the pink sweater away. He kissed her while he unfastened her jeans, slid his hand beneath the waistband and made the zipper crawl down tooth by tooth as he moved his hand over her firm belly. There was a band of lace and a triangle of cotton, but he felt the satin softness of skin kept covered, and his fingertips detected the intimate protection of springy hair. It was like plotting a course. He'd assured himself of his destination, but he didn't want to shorten the journey. He pushed her jeans over her hips, and she lifted one foot at a time so he could remove them.

She looked smaller now than he'd imagined. His hands could almost span her waist. He dropped one knee to the floor and tried it, and suddenly it wasn't important to her that her room lacked feminine frills. She had a female waist, female hips. He moved his hands over them and rested his forehead between the lacy cups of her bra.

"You're so small," he whispered.

"Is that bad?"

"It scares me. I've never...been with such a small woman."

"Small but strong. I build roads."

"*I* build roads. And I have a habit of blasting my way through."

She raked her fingers through his thick hair. "I'll show you where to set the charges."

He unfastened the clasp between her breasts and pushed one more bit of fabric away before he came to his feet to cover her breasts again, this time with his hands. He claimed her mouth with a caressing kiss, moving his lips over hers as he moved his thumbs over her skin, seeking her response. With her arms around his neck she filled her lungs with air, hoping to give him a little more of her to hold and touch. The roughened pads of his thumbs found her nipples and whisked over them like pieces of corduroy polishing cloth, making them into small beads. She felt her nipples' new luster in the way they tingled, but the sudden shrinkage made her groan into his mouth.

"Don't ask me to set charges on such perfect little peaks," he whispered hotly. "I never knew a woman could be so—"

"Please don't say small."

"Delicate."

"I don't want to be delicate."

"What do you want to be?"

"Voluptuous."

He moved quickly, hiding his amusement by lifting her high off the floor. He had to find the bathroom by instinct, because his face was bracketed by her breasts.

"I want you to be wet, the way you were by the creek." He first turned the light on, then the shower. "I couldn't help wishing for *naked* and wet." He shed his jeans quickly, watching her all the while. Her eyes never left his face.

It was he who removed the last of her clothing, sliding his hands over her hips, and he who orchestrated the shower. The water was hot, and the soap made them slick, so that belly slid against belly, thigh against thigh. He moved his hands over her, making small swirls of suds and listening for the catch in her breath. She tried to do likewise, but he'd conveyed her to a higher plane, and her initiative waned as she gave in to her irresistible responses. When he slipped his hand between her thighs, she gasped and relied on his arm for support. He'd located the critical crevice, and he wondered how tenderly he could manage to set his charge there.

Steam filled the tiny room. Finally, Megan stepped out of the tub and into Sage's waiting arms. Using the tip of his tongue, he sipped water from her face and neck. She felt behind her back for the towel bar, but he reached past her, one arm on either side, and anchored the towel in place. At the same time he moved his mouth over her breasts, suckling each nipple in turn until she gave a sultry moan. Then he kissed his way downward.

She was slick, like a water slide, and he'd begun his descent. "So good," he whispered against her dewy skin. "Sweet and hot, like the perfect dessert."

She had no thought of stopping him, even when he reached the dense curls that shielded her femininity. She had no thoughts at all. There was only the spicy feeling rippling from the point of the contact to all the reaches of her body. She braced her hands on his shoulders and chanted his name as the pleasurable throbbing intensified. He rose through the mist and pinned her to the wall, sliding his body over hers.

"Was it enough?" he asked as his lips drifted through the damp sheen on her forehead.

She rolled her head back and forth against the wall. "I'm afraid your tongue's too small."

He lifted his head and saw the glaze in her eyes, the wistful smile on her kiss-reddened lips. His laughter started deep within his chest and emerged as a wicked sound. He took her hand and slid it down the front of his body. "You wanna try this on for size?"

"If we do it right here, you won't have to worry about opening up that pesky—"

He groaned, shutting her up and cutting off his own curse with a hungry kiss. Steam followed them into the bedroom. Sage lay down and pulled her into his arms, and he kept her mindless while he took his precautions. His body alone filled her senses—its hard planes and sleek skin, the heat of his breath and the pounding of his heart in time with her own. Finally he raised her knees to ease his entry and filled her so far beyond the physical bounds that she wept for his tenderness even as she arched her hips to help him make the explosion happen.

When it was done, he kissed away her tears. In the silence, he thought of all the things that might have brought them on. When he finally asked "Did I hurt you?" it came in a hoarse whisper that embarrassed him because it sounded so unmanly in his own ears.

"I can't imagine being hurt by you," she said. "I didn't know . . . anything like that was possible."

He allowed a slow smile. "It fit, then?"

"Like the key to a lock." She slid her hand along her side and cupped her own breast. "I know I'm small. I'd like to have long hair, like Regina's, and breasts like—"

"There's nothing wrong with delicate." He rolled to his back and gathered her in his arms. "I thought my heart would burst when I saw how small and pretty you were."

"I thought you were disappointed."

He kissed the top of her head. "Were you disappointed?"

"In you? Never. You're perfect."

"No, I'm not," he protested. "I'm far from perfect. You've got to know that, and it's got to be okay with you. I can't be perfect."

"Nearly perfect, then." She traced a line along his jaw. "You've come so far. I've watched how hard you work."

"I've got a long way to go, Megan." He looked down, searching for understanding in those tranquil blue eyes. He saw pure satisfaction. "I've never made love to a friend before," he confided. "Hell, I'm not sure I've ever made love before."

"What do you mean? You were mar—"

"I've had a lot of sex," he said quickly. "I've screwed a lot of women. I didn't do that to you. I made love to you."

She smiled. "I know."

He held her close and tucked her head under his chin. "I made love to someone I care about. God, it felt good." He swallowed hard, trying to soothe the burning in his throat. "Your tears scared the hell out of me. I thought I'd done something wrong."

"You were so gentle, Sage." She kissed the base of his throat. "You keep telling me how bad you've been, but all I see is good. You've wrestled with the bad things, and you've won."

She made him feel so good that he couldn't argue with her. He couldn't bring himself to tell her just then how he struggled every day, and how he would go on struggling for the rest of his life. He wanted to be good to her always. That much he knew.

"I still want your friendship first," he told her. "Without that, we've got nothing."

"I know." She leaned back to look at him. His good looks always stunned her—his black hair, still damp from their shower, his dark, enigmatic eyes, and his deeply tanned face with its hard, angular features. She touched his lower lip with her forefinger. "So tell me things friends tell each other. From the very beginning."

"From the beginning, huh?" He nipped at her finger, then smiled. "Well . . . in the beginning, there was a harrowing buckboard ride. My mother was in labor, and my father was trying to get her to the clinic. She'd already delivered at home six times, and the doctor had warned her not to try it again. She was getting too old for that stuff."

"A buckboard ride?" she asked. "We're talking about your mother, now, not your grandmother."

"A buckboard ride," he confirmed. "We were, uh, between cars. About the time I started school, my dad had a Model A."

"A Model A!"

He reached for the chenille spread that had managed to work its way to the foot of the bed, and he tossed it over them. "You don't believe me? I'm telling you, a buckboard and a Model A. Now, this is the true story of my birth, so show some respect."

She made herself comfortable, pillowing her head on his shoulder and wondering whether she was really in for a tall tale. "Okay. Your father was driving the buckboard."

"And she kept yelling at him to go faster, and he kept saying they should have stayed home." He used his free hand to follow the motion of the story in the air above their heads. "So, they're bumping along, and the back wheel falls off the axle." The heel of his hand skidded to a stop in the middle of his chest.

"Are you sure you're not confusing this with the pickup?"

"Of course I'm sure. I've heard the damn story a hundred times. Between contractions my mom had to get down from the buckboard and shove the wheel back on while my dad held the axle up. 'Course, he couldn't drive it 'cause the burr was busted. He set the brake, unhitched the team and got back up there in time to catch me coming out of the chute."

Megan laughed so hard that the words, "You're making . . . all this . . . up," were barely intelligible.

"Hell, I could never invent anything this good," he assured her. "So my mom says to my dad, 'Husband, I have given you another son.'"

"Oh, come on."

"Well, words to that effect." His shoulders shook with silent laughter. "By the time the whole scene was edited for the retelling, that was her line. She never thought the story was too funny until it came to that line.''

"I can imagine."

"So then he says, 'What name have you chosen for this lusty, strapping man-child?'"

"Give me a break," Megan groaned.

"So that's when she always turned to me with the real solemn look and said, 'I had your name all picked out, son. It was going to be Sampson. But you didn't lift a finger to help me with that wheel. I looked around me—nothing but jackrabbits and sage as far as the eye could see—and I looked down at you, and I knew who you were.'"

She shifted toward him, laid her arm over his chest and savored the sound of his name. "Sage."

"Uh-uh." He put his lips close to her ear and whispered, "Jackrabbit."

"Oh, you!" She pinched his side and discovered that he was ticklish. "A-ha! Now I know your weak spot."

He held her hand still and flashed his wicked grin. "Use it against me and I'll find every one of yours."

"How come you weren't this funny when we first met?"

"How come you weren't this friendly when we first met?"

The softness they saw in one another's eyes only hinted at the answers each chose to keep for now.

I would have been, if I had trusted you as I do now.
I would have been, if I had loved you as I do now.

Megan snuggled against him again. "How much of that story is true?"

"Nearly every word. It was my mother's favorite kid story."

"Is she dead now?"

"Mmm-hmm. So's my dad."

"It's a beautiful name," she said quietly. "It's a wonderful story."

"You know what I just discovered?" He turned the thought over in his mind for a moment just to be sure of it. "I can tell that story just as well sober as I can half-crocked."

"Better, maybe."

"Better, maybe," he agreed. He turned his head and kissed the top of hers. "You're the best damn audience a guy could ask for, Megan McBride."

"Most gullible?"

"Most eager," he told her. She lifted her head to see whether he was laughing at her and found only the softness in his eyes. "You're the first woman I've told that story to." He combed his fingers through her damp hair. "I really like this."

"What?"

"Lying here with you. Holding each other and just talking...touching."

"But you've been..."

"No." He laid a finger over her lips and shook his head. "No. This is new for me, Megan. I'm not half-shot and cocky as hell, and I wasn't looking for somebody to get off with." He slid his hand over her shoulder and down the length of her back. "I can't believe how good this feels."

"You were afraid to tell me what you were looking for."

"I was afraid it didn't exist. At least, not for me. I was afraid I didn't have...what you said...something to share with someone like you."

"I wish I had met you first," she said, and she kissed his shoulder. It was hers to kiss, she thought recklessly, and it should never have been anyone else's. "Before your wife. Before the other women."

"We couldn't have had what we've had tonight. If I'd had you then, you wouldn't be here now."

"Things might have been different."

"You couldn't have changed me, Megan. I had to do that for myself." He lifted his head to look at her face. Her pretty face. She was so confident in her ability to make things right. "I'm glad you came along when you did. I think I was ready for you."

"Well, almost." She propped her chin on his shoulder and hiked a teasing eyebrow. "You were after you stopped at Kessler's."

With a chuckle he dropped his head back on the pillow. "I'm doing good." Rolling his head to the side allowed him to see her face again. "See? That's a prime example. Years ago, I would have knocked you up without thinking twice."

"Sage! I . . . I wouldn't have let you."

He frowned. "You're not on the pill, are you?"

"N-no. I . . . had no reason to be."

"You got something else stashed around here?" She shook her head. "It was my idea, then, wasn't it?" She nodded, feeling foolish. "See? I really am doing good." He touched her cheek and whispered, "I hate the thought of hurting you."

She closed her eyes and laid her cheek against his shoulder again. "I didn't think. I just wanted us to make love."

He hugged her close, grateful for her trust and pleased with himself for proving worthy, at least tonight. "Tell me your story, Megan."

"Mine isn't as good as yours."

"It must be. Megan sounds like somebody they should write a song about."

"It's my grandmother's name," she said matter-of-factly. "My sister got my other grandmother's name. My parents live in Pierre, but I don't see much of them anymore."

"Why not?" He figured he knew why, but he wanted her to tell him.

"I wish my father could go to a Medicine Wheel meeting," she said quietly. "If he would just stop drinking once and for all—"

"There is no 'once and for all,' Megan. There's no 'happily ever after.' There's just one day at a time."

She smoothed her hand over his chest. "Four years is a lot of one days."

"Sometimes a day is too much. Sometimes, when it's really bad, when all you can think about is where the nearest bottle is—sometimes you tell yourself to hold on for another minute. And then you figure maybe you can go one more."

"Do you have days like that?"

"Not as often as I used to, but, yeah. Some."

"What do you do?"

"I go to a meeting. I find someone to talk to—someone like me. I try to sweat it out in the lodge. I pray."

"Could you ever... come to me?"

"Uh-uh." He felt her disappointment, and he rubbed her back, hoping the disappointment would melt away. He needed her acceptance. "You're not an alcoholic, Megan. You can't take care of us. But you can care. Don't cut yourself off from your father. There are no perfect people. We're all struggling. Tell him that you want him to get help."

"He won't listen."

"Maybe not, but it's all you can do."

"Look at all *you* do." She rose up as though she were going to accuse him of something. "You're trying to get a whole bar closed down. Aren't you looking out for other people?"

"I'm hoping we'll start looking out for ourselves as a community. When I came back from treatment with the idea for Medicine Wheel, I felt like one hand clapping. Pretty soon we had a little group. We're growing, and we're getting healthy enough to try to make our community healthy."

"When's the next hearing?" she asked. "I want to be there."

He pulled her toward him, and she lay back down in his arms. "I don't think that's a good idea anymore, Megan."

"Why not? Just standing by you isn't caretaking, is it?"

"There have been... threats. Taylor stands to lose one business, maybe two, if Regina gets the store going. I don't want him to try to get to me by...maybe trying to hurt you.''

''He threatened you?''

''It's just something you need to be aware of.'' He cupped her breast with a protective hand. ''This kind of sharing is nice, but I don't want to share my enemies with you.''

''I'm going to that hearing,'' she insisted.

''Whatever you say.'' Turning on his side, he adjusted her in his arms. ''It's stopped raining,'' he told her. ''If we went to sleep right now, we might get in four hours before daybreak, which is when we'd better get out to the site.''

She nuzzled his neck. ''I could make do with three and a half. I've been going to bed early all my life.''

''What for?''

''Resting up for tonight.''

He rolled on top of her and hooked his leg over hers. He was more than ready. ''If you were so damn sure of yourself, why didn't you stop at the drugstore before you came to get me?''

''Came to get—''

Megan's protest was lost in Sage's kiss.

Chapter 11

Sage's cryptic comments about the threats against him worried Megan, but he showed no concern for himself. His only·fear seemed to be for her. She decided to pay Pete Petersen a visit. He seemed to understand local politics, and she thought he was probably within earshot of most of the local rumors, as well.

Pete still hadn't oiled the springs in his desk chair. They creaked as he leaned back, linking his fingers over his stomach. "Sounds to me like you've developed more than a professional interest in Sage Parker."

"We've been working together all summer," she reminded him as she uncrossed her legs and resettled herself in her chair. "It can't be too surprising that we've become friends." She recrossed her legs from the other side.

"Not surprising at all," Pete returned with a smile.

"Besides that, Sage's pickup was sabotaged on the site."

His eyebrows shot up, his interest piqued. "Sabotaged?"

"The lug nuts were loosened on one of the tires. The whole wheel fell off."

"Anybody hurt?" Pete asked as he leaned forward in concern.

"Sage might have been. He nearly went over an embankment. Frankly, I think he knows more about it than he's told me."

Pete picked up a pencil and tapped the eraser against his desk pad. "Well, you asked me if I thought somebody might be out to get him on this liquor license thing, and I guess you've answered your own question. Sounds like somebody is."

"Taylor?"

"Could be." Pete tossed the pencil aside in disgust. "Taylor's an opportunist. A taker, like so many of the people who've beaten a path to the reservations to make a buck. They've cheated these people out of land, food, program money, lease checks—you name it. It's been going on for over a hundred years. And they always seem to be taking with one hand and peddling whiskey with the other."

"If someone stands up to them, is he likely to be...punished somehow?"

"Your friend might be found dead alongside the road." He punctuated the news with a clucking sound.

"I've been here almost twenty years. I remember one guy who tried to blow the whistle on a fishy cattle-buying deal. Government program, tribe was buying cattle, some of the records didn't jibe. After this guy got shot at on the highway a few times, he decided he'd forgotten how to add. And the tribe figured if they didn't take what they got, they wouldn't get anything. That's the history of this place. That's why people tend to just let things go."

Megan tightened her grip on the arms of her chair. "Do you hear anything about . . . how much support Sage has?"

"Oh, yeah, Sage is the talk of the town. He's either a saint or a sinner, depending on who you talk to. Some people are standing neutral on the issue itself, but there's no neutral ground where Sage is concerned."

"He, um, he thinks I might be threatened, too."

"Why? Because you've gone to a couple of council sessions? A Medicine Wheel meeting or two?" Megan shot him a scowl. "I'm the one who gave you the information, remember? I haven't heard too much talk about you, but everybody knows who you are. Around here, people see a man and a woman together more than once, they draw conclusions."

Good, she thought. Let them. If they want to shoot at him, they can shoot at me, too. She caught Pete's intuitive smile, and she returned it with pride.

"He's no saint, Megan, but he's a damn good man. He's been working at it for a good long time now, and he's doing fine." He bobbed his head as he repeated the conviction. "He's doing just fine."

"He's helping people. I saw that at the meeting."

Pete leaned back in his chair and clasped his hands behind his head. "Do you think you might be interested in a civil service job with the BIA? I've got a guy transferring out in September, and I'm looking at retirement soon myself. Be a good future in it for you."

Megan raised a speculative eyebrow. "I guess it wouldn't hurt to fill out an application."

Pete took her to the local café for hamburgers. It was after seven when she unlocked the door to her pickup. As she opened it, she caught a glimpse of a stern face in the side mirror. The unfriendly look in the dark eyes was chilling. Megan turned slowly, her mind spinning with possibilities that she didn't much like.

"Hello, Regina."

"I'm looking for Sage."

Megan's eyes narrowed as she frowned. "He isn't with me."

"I thought you might be with him," Regina said flatly. "We have a meeting scheduled for seven-thirty tonight. We're helping them start a group here like the one we've got going in Red Calf."

"Then I'm sure he'll be here. I left the site early. Sage did say he had a meeting tonight, but he didn't mention where."

The look on Regina's face betrayed her doubt. Let her think what she wanted, Megan decided. She wasn't following Sage. If she had known Sage planned to be in Pine Ridge, she would have planned her visit for another day. He might ask questions about her reason for visiting Pete, and her answer might be construed as "caretaking." Megan was tired of trying to figure out what the word really meant.

"He's always early," Regina said. "He always makes sure there's coffee, and we set up the chairs."

Megan laughed. "You could float a battleship in the coffee that man consumes." She touched Regina's arm, hoping the gesture would be taken as friendly. "I'm sure he stopped off to change his clothes, and he probably had a couple of chores to do or something. He's bound to be along soon."

Regina seemed to be intimidated by Megan's hand. She lowered her eyes and stood quite still. "I just thought you might have come together."

Megan dropped her hand, but she felt something more genuine reaching toward the woman from within herself. "We didn't. Medicine Wheel is something I . . . would never interfere with, Regina. Never. Sage asked me to go to a meeting and see how it worked. I'm glad I did. I understand why it's so important to him."

"It's his lifeline," Regina said. "It can't be replaced by a woman."

Megan felt a tightening in her throat. "I know that."

"Good."

Regina turned to walk away, but Megan spoke her name, and she turned back. "How are you doing?" Megan asked gently.

Regina nodded, and the tension dropped from her shoulders as she sighed. "Okay. It's hard," she admitted. "With the children. My two older ones took it hard." Her eyes grew cloudy with emotion. "I'm doing okay."

"Your husband was a good worker," Megan offered, choosing not to mention any exceptions. "I enjoyed having him on the crew." With another nod, Regina accepted the bid for a truce.

Megan backed her pickup away from the curb, but before she had it in gear, she heard someone call her name. Pete left his car idling on the opposite side of the street with the door standing open. His awkward attempt at a jog would have seemed funny if he hadn't had such a grave expression on his face.

He braced himself in her open window and struggled to catch his breath. "I just heard some bad news ... about Sage."

The smell of it was the worst part now. Flesh on fire. It was more pungent than the acrid smell of wood smoke or burning hay. Sage's eyes stung, and his gut roiled. The air around him was heavy with that smell. He dropped his forehead against his fingertips and rubbed his eyes with the heels of his hands, hoping to find enough moisture in them to relieve the stinging. The heat had left them dry.

With his eyes closed there was only the swirl of sounds—the crackle and hiss, the call for water, the shifting of timber. And the smell. He saw Jackie's rotting flesh behind his eyelids and imagined the wild-eyed colt with its spotted hide ablaze. He tasted the bile rising in the back of his throat, and he wished his stomach would settle down. He would have been grateful just for that.

Another beam gave way behind him. He turned to watch the charred bones of his dream clatter one against the another, and, like dominoes, they finally knocked each other down. Within moments the subfloor gave way, and the smoking rubble collapsed into its own cement grave.

Sage watched the rural volunteer fire department reorganize its efforts to attack the barn from a different angle. There was little left to save. They'd kept the fire from spreading across the prairie, which was a commendable feat. The house had gone quickly, but bright orange flames from the barn still licked the evening sky. Twilight had given the horizon a shrinking red rim, and the first few stars had claimed their places in the heavens.

Sage wondered where his place was since heaven had no use for him. He'd tried to change, and there were places in him that were still raw from the effort. But he'd made the effort. He'd shivered and sweated with it. He'd stumbled and dragged himself on his belly until he found his legs could hold him again. It must have been an unforgivably disgusting sight. Why else would God have turned His head while some son of a bitch set a torch to the only real dream he'd ever had?

He lay back on the hood of his pickup, where somebody had insisted he sit and rest for a while. He'd seen the smoke on his way home, and he'd had a sinking feeling well before he saw the blaze. Several neighbors and one of the fire pickups were already on the scene. Despair had turned to rage, and he'd been a madman for a while there. He'd probably scared the hell out of them at first, when he'd tried to get into the barn. Then he'd settled down and helped with the hoses and the buckets until the nausea had over-whelmed him.

What had he done? There was supposed to be for-giveness up there, wasn't there? A single star winked at him. It was all a terrific joke, wasn't it? It was the ultimate tease. Destiny enjoyed letting you think you had a say. He'd had the audacity to believe things could change. If people wanted to drink, they'd drink. Hell, he knew that.

And he knew better than to think a good woman could love Sage Parker. He'd had his chance, and he wasn't supposed to get another one. He'd been puffed up with pride again just because he'd nailed a few boards together and bought a few cows. And then he'd taken a woman. He wasn't supposed to have a woman. He wasn't good enough for any woman. Women meant family, and he wasn't supposed to have that, either.

The smell was proof. He was fond of saying he'd been to hell and back. Now he knew different. Hell was the end of the line.

"How're you doing, Sage?"

He sat up. It took him a moment to think of his neighbor's name. Old Bernie Richards. He'd known the man since he was a kid. Bernie's gray hair was covered with soot; maybe that was why Sage hadn't recognized him. And he hadn't really heard the ques-tion.

"You okay, Sage?" Bernie laid a hand on Sage's shoulder in an attempt to cut through the blank stare. "This is a hell of a thing. I think you oughta stay with somebody for a while, son." Bernie waited for a reaction, but got none. "How 'bout your brother George? He still around?"

Sage shook his head. "Moved to Montana." He covered the old man's hand with his own. "I'm okay, Bernie. I appreciate your help."

"You can sure stay with us," Bernie offered.

"I've still got the trailer." His stony gaze strayed to the barn again. "I'll be fine."

"Well, I just wanted to warn you. A couple of young fellas got a bottle going around over there." He nodded at a trio taking a break near the corral. "You keep your head on straight, son. You hear?"

Sage stared at the small party that was being held in honor of his barn-burning.

"You got any insurance, son?"

His gaze was riveted on the three men. "No. No insurance."

"That's the hell of it. Who can pay for it nowadays?" Bernie patted Sage's shoulder. "Not much more I can do tonight, Sage. This is gonna burn itself out now. Lucky it didn't spread."

"Yeah. Lucky."

"Anything you need—"

"Thanks, Bernie."

He had no idea what they were drinking, but he could taste it. His throat was raw from the smoke, and his mouth was dry. He turned his head quickly and tried to fix his mind on something else. There was the trailer. One of his saddles was in the bedroom. Most of his tools were in the back of the pickup. He still had a job. He needed Medicine Wheel. Now. There was a meeting going on right now, and he needed . . .

"I'll bet you could use a drink right about now."

It cut deep, like an electrical shock. Sage pressed his lips together and turned slowly, trying to remember how to refuse. He wasn't even sure who this man was, but he knew one of the guys he was drinking with. Lonnie Crow. Sage remembered drinking with Lonnie, too.

"You've had a tough night. One drink won't hurt."

Sage tried to ignore the bottle. "Did you come with the fire fighters?"

The man stuck out his hand. "Gordon Brown. I came with Lonnie. He's a friend of Chet's, and Chet's a volunteer."

Sage caught himself watching the man take a long pull on the bottle. In the dark it was hard to tell much about him. He wore a cowboy hat and sounded pretty South Dakota. Sage could feel the potent liquid roll down the man's throat as he watched him swallow.

Gordon wiped his mouth on his sleeve and leaned on the hood of the pickup, setting the bottle in front of him. "This is a damn shame, Sage. Lonnie said you did most of the work here yourself."

Sage took a deep breath and held it. Whiskey. He could smell it. It smelled a hell of a lot better than burning horseflesh. He watched his hand close over the neck of the bottle.

The first taste singed his tongue and burned going down. He filled his mouth with it again and made his peace with it. He'd screwed up somehow, and he was being punished. He thought he'd changed, but his insides were still filled with scum. Something that tasted like lye might clean that out for him.

It was hard to see the extent of the damage in the dark, but the barn was obviously a complete loss. As Megan's pickup neared the trailer, she could see that the basement of the house had become a firepit, and she felt physically sick. She remembered Sage's imposing figure on the roof top and the halo effect the sun had given him. With two separate fires there was no pretense of an accident. She left her pickup near the trailer and went searching for him.

He saw her coming. His first instinct was to hide the bottle. His brain buzzed from the effects of the whiskey, but he hadn't reached the stage of not caring about anything. He wouldn't enjoy having her see him this way. It would be like getting beaten up right in front of her. But his instincts were overruled by a greater need to be honest with her—to let her see the truth.

When she saw him sitting there, she mouthed his name and hurried toward him. Her look of distress was fixed on his face, and she saw nothing else. Waves of regret washed over him. He would have given anything at that moment to be the man she thought she was running to. Then he remembered he had nothing to offer up in trade.

He slid down from the pickup hood, leaving the open fifth standing at his back in plain view. Still she saw nothing but him as she slipped her arms around him and laid her ahead against his chest. She asked no questions, gave him no words of sympathy. She simply held him.

Tradition said there should have been an argument right at the outset. The sooner he could get angry at her, the sooner he could stop feeling like a piece of trash. If he worked it right, he could convince her that his failure was hers, too, and he could add her contempt to his list of reasons to finish the bottle. But she was ignorant of the tradition. In her mind she was still holding the man she'd said goodbye to earlier in the day.

There was no place to put his arms but around her shoulders. He felt her shudder against him and hoped to God she wasn't crying. He had no comfort to offer. He wanted to crawl inside her and shut the rest of the world away. Maybe he could walk away from the bottle. Maybe Megan would forgive him this one trespass and take his pain away by that very act.

His shirt reeked of smoke, but she buried her face against it anyway. If she'd been there sooner, she could have helped him fight the fire, and then the smoke from his home would have permeated her clothing, as well. She imagined him battling the blaze and finally had the presence of mind to ask, "Are you hurt?"

"Hurt?" he repeated, confused. Shouldn't that have been, Are you drunk?

She looked up at his soot-smeared face and saw the glazed expression in his eyes. She ran her hands along his arms, and he winced when she came to his hands. They examined them together, finding scrapes and blisters. "You're burned," she said as evenly as she could manage. "We need to get you to a doctor."

He found it strange that he hadn't noticed his
hands, when just looking at them now seemed to make
them hurt. "Must've happened when I tried to get the
barn door open. Tried to get the horses..." He lowered his hands as the account became a sickened
groan.

"Horses," Megan whispered.

"I always leave that side door open during the day
so they can go in for shade. There's a latch that holds
it open—I *always*..." He tipped his head back and
searched the sky for help, but none was there. Blink-
ing hard, he swallowed the sting in his throat and told
himself to hang on to what was left of his dignity. Finally he risked looking down at her face. "The mare
and her colt were in the barn, Megan. That door had
been bolted shut."

"Oh, my God," came her thin whisper.

"I know I didn't shut that door." He'd gone over it
in his mind a dozen times, retracing his steps, but this
was the first time he'd said it aloud. "I filled the water tank this morning. I fed them, locked up the storage closet and secured that latch." He'd broken a
sweat just talking about it. In an impatient gesture he
wiped his brow with his sleeve. "You could smell the
kerosene. Hell, I don't even keep any kerosene out
there."

"Sage, it was set. We'll tell the authorities. They'll
find out who did this." She had both his shoulders in
her grip when she noticed the bitter-sweet scent. Her
eyes widened as she stiffened. "Sage?"

He reached behind him and slid the dark bottle to
his side, watching her all the while. She blanched. He

was sure of it. There in the darkness she lost all color in her face. Some sinister need to shock her overcame him, and he tipped the bottle to his mouth and sucked the stuff down greedily.

"Sage, what are you doing!"

He set the bottle down, wiped his mouth on the back of his hand and gave her a cold smile. "I'm getting drunk."

"You can't do that," she said, trying to keep the sound of panic from laying claim to her voice.

"It's been a while, but I think I remember how it's done."

He started to raise the bottle again, and she grabbed his arm. "You don't need that, Sage. You're through with that. You've beaten it!"

He transferred the whiskey into his other hand and took another drink. Pressing his lips together, he stared her down. "Don't ever try to separate a drunk from his bottle, Megan. You can get hurt that way."

"You'd never hurt me."

"You can't be sure of that," he warned. "You can't be sure of anything in this life."

"And you're *not* a drunk anymore, so stop calling yourself that."

"Oh yeah?" His laughter sounded cruel. "That's where you're wrong, baby. You're in way over your head, and there's a hell of a storm brewing." He latched on to her upper arm, and the pain that flashed in his eyes had origins far deeper than his blistered skin. "I know you can swim, Megan," he said, desperately struggling with the gravel in his throat. "Remember? Head for higher ground. There's nothing left here."

"You're here," she whispered in a voice full of tears.

He touched her cheek with raw fingers. "I'm going under."

"You've got a lot of friends, Sage." They both turned toward the voice of reason, which came from Pete Petersen. "They're not going to let you down. This doesn't end here."

Sage looked back at Megan, his eyes suddenly cold again. "What? You brought reinforcements?"

"Pete was the one who told me—"

Another car arrived, and two doors slammed shut. Sage peered over Megan's head. "Damn," Sage muttered between clenched teeth. "What's next? The Seventh Cavalry?" He dropped his hands and sidled away from her, glaring. "Where's your bugle, baby? Let's have the whole show."

The approaching feet swished in the grass. Megan turned to find that Regina had brought another group member. Lonnie, Gordon and Chet were converging from another direction.

"Sage, let's get your hands taken care of," Megan urged. There was no disguising her anxiety anymore. It rolled down her cheeks in glittering tears.

"Yeah, let's." In defiance he splashed whiskey over the worst of his burns. He sucked his breath between clenched teeth and took masochistic pleasure in the wild stinging. "There. All taken care of."

"Hey, don't waste it," Gordon called as he sauntered through the tall grass. "That's good stuff."

"Give it back to them, Sage," Regina said quietly. "Talk to us. Let's have the circle right out here."

Sage glanced from one face to another, then past them to the handful of firemen still soaking the smouldering timbers of his barn. He felt like an animal caught in a trap. They all wanted pieces of him, and if he stood there much longer, they would get their wish. He'd shatter.

"We're gonna take off, Sage." Sage swung his head toward Lonnie. *Take off* reverberated in his brain. "Thought we'd hit some spots. It's been a hell of a thirsty night."

"We got room for you, if you wanna come along." Gordon's offer rolled off his tongue like a bolt of silk.

Sage made his move.

"Please don't go, Sage."

The voice was small and pretty and wet with womanly tears. He got behind the wheel of his pickup and kept his eyes on the remains of the barn as he shut the door.

The little group huddled together and watched the lights of one pickup trail the other.

"He's in no condition to drive," Megan said. "He won't be hard to find. There aren't that many bars—"

"Don't do it, Megan," Pete warned. "He's on his own now."

"But he'll get into trouble."

"You can't prevent that," Pete told her.

"He's in trouble now." Regina's resignation was chilling.

"We can't just stand here and watch him do this to himself," Megan insisted.

"The best thing you can do is call the police." Megan looked horrified, but Pete continued. "They'll stop him from hurting himself, or someone else."

"I . . . couldn't do that to him," she said.

"Then you haven't learned anything." Disgusted by the white woman's weakness, Regina headed back to her car.

Megan felt lost. "Pete, I can't sit idly by—"

He laid a hand on her shoulder. "Go home. Get some sleep. I'll take care of the call. And if he comes to you, don't try to talk to him when he's drunk. You won't get anywhere."

Feeling shell-shocked, Megan allowed herself to be escorted to her pickup.

The face in the mirror was ghastly. A night of little sleep had left its shadows beside traces of soot. Cavernous eyes seemed to lack a human soul. A puffiness reminiscent of death made Sage turn his eyes downward toward the sink. It was a sight that would drive young children to hide behind their mothers' legs. His own often had. Taking both sides of the sink gingerly in his hands, he lowered his entire face into the basin of icy water. Much to his dismay, he hadn't drowned during the night. He had half a mind to correct fate's error there in the sink.

On his way back up he bumped his head on the faucet. He muttered a curse. The bump was only a small insult to add to the injury he'd already heaped on his own head. His hair was plastered around his face, and the water rushed to form a single stream over his square chin. He looked down and considered his hands, which reminded him of rashers of bacon. The aching intensified as he eased them, palms up, into the water. His fingers trembled, and he saw the bacon curling, bubbling up in a cast-iron skillet. The mere image of cooking produced an imaginary odor that turned his stomach.

Minutes passed, and the cold water dulled the pain in his hands as he listened to Elmer Fudd harangue the "cwazy wabbit." Hell, he must have left the TV on all night. He pulled the black rubber stopper up by its chain and leaned his forearms on the edge of the sink as he watched the water eddy toward the drain. Then the pint bottle on the back of the commode caught his eye.

It was in his hand before he thought about reaching. Funny he hadn't drained the bottle the night before. Apparently it hadn't taken as much as it used to to make him pass out. He studied the label. Maybe he didn't know anything about wine, but he had good taste in whiskey. But the taste in his mouth wasn't good. He was afraid that if he opened it in front of the mirror, he would find a coating of mold. Whiskey killed bacteria, he told himself as his mouth yearned toward the bottle. Whiskey...

He struck the bottle against the side of the sink and watched the brown liquid slide over the shattered glass and down the drain. Whiskey would kill him, and he didn't want to die. The realization made him quiver. He wanted life. Despite all the losses he'd sustained in one chaotic night, he would live. He *would* live.

Picking up the pieces might be almost as tricky as cleaning up the mess he'd just made. He sliced his hand with the first shard of glass, and he saw that he was bound to bleed a little. What did he expect? Bleeding occasionally was part of life. Besides, he was a little short on dexterity just now. It might be a week or so before he could manage a hammer again.

The knock at the door echoed the clatter of glass as he tossed it in the waste basket. He jerked his head around and took a quick survey. Hot Springs. Easy Rider Motel. It was definitely a step down from the Arrowhead. Bugs Bunny was in black and white, and the picture was rolling. A lot like his gut.

After the second knock he yelled, "Yeah, I'm coming." He was going to add "Keep your shirt on," but he realized he was missing his. He'd slept in sooty jeans, and the bedding showed it. He flipped the bedspread over the sheets and picked his shirt up off the floor. No doubt the manager had come to give him hell over the TV, which he switched off on his way to the door.

It was Megan. He stared at her dumbly, unable to draw breath. She looked tired, but her eyes were clear; her face looked fresh, and everything about her struck him as immaculate. The Easy Rider Motel was not her turf.

"You look like hell," she told him.

"Thanks." He wanted to laugh, but he hadn't rallied that far yet. Getting enough air into his lungs for a one word response hed been a major accomplishment. "Come on in."

The room was small, dark and oppressive. Faded flowered wallpaper was peeling above the bed, and the sculpturing in the green carpet had worn to fuzz. The pronounced smell of whiskey prepared Megan for signs of an all-night party, but she saw none.

"How did you find me?"

"Your pickup is one of a kind. I wasn't looking. I was just on my way to work. Frankly, I'm surprised you're not in jail."

He saw the judgment in her eyes, saw how the sight of him sickened her. He felt cold. His shame had left him naked, and her eyes chilled him. He groped for a comeback. "Just lucky, I guess."

"Pete said we should call the police just to get you off the road."

"He was right. You should have."

"I thought he was going to."

"He probably called the Indian police. They don't have any jurisdiction off the reservation." He raised his hand to offer her a chair, and blood dripped on the carpet.

"Oh my God, what have you done?" Her hands shot out reflexively, and she grabbed his arm.

"I cut myself on a bottle." Her eyes flew up to his as she took charge of his hand, cradling it in both of hers. "Not intentionally," he added quickly. "If I wanted to do myself in, I'd cut off my aching head."

"Sage, your hands need attention. Have you washed them?"

"Yeah, sort of." He let her lead him back to the sink because it was her attention he craved. Even if she cared only for his hands, it was an acknowledgment of his humanity. The mirror had suggested to him that he might be something less.

"I have a first aid kit in the car. Let me get it."

By the time she returned, he'd washed his hands with soap and water, and they were dripping to form a puddle near his bare feet. She told him to sit on the bed, while she washed her own hands and then pulled up a chair, lining her knees up with his. After laying his hands palms-up on a towel in her lap, she blew his skin dry. When he told her how good it felt, she refused to look up and let him see any commiseration on her part. She wanted to be angry, not so much because he'd started drinking, but because he hadn't stopped when she'd asked him to.

She painstakingly dabbed antiseptic cream over his damaged skin and bandaged the cut at the base of his thumb. "This is the main reason I stopped when I saw your pickup."

By that time he felt up to a chuckle. "You wanted to make sure I washed my hands?"

"You should have seen a doctor," she insisted, still fussing over his injuries.

"It took a lot of guts for you to stop here. You didn't know how bad off I might have been...or whether you'd find someone else in this bed with me."

She glanced up at him. "I wasn't thinking that way."

"Neither was I. But you had no way of knowing, did you?"

She lowered her eyes and shook her head.

"After what we...after the other night, I can understand why you're here. But you can't be running after me when...if this happens. Before long you'll be as crazy as I am.''

Megan took a deep breath as she covered his wrists with her cool hands. ''This is something I can do, Sage. I can see the injury here, and I can tend to it. The other...'' Her eyes betrayed her fear. ''I want to help you, but I don't know how.''

He lifted his hands, and she let hers slide away. ''This much is fine. I would have had a hard time doing this on my own. Otherwise...'' He shook his head. ''You can't fix it for me, Megan, any more than you could for Jackie.''

''You're not like Jackie,'' she insisted.

''I *am* like Jackie. Look!'' He held his hands up in front of her face. ''I'm flesh and blood, just like he was. I'm an alcoholic, just like he was. And if I choose to, I can lie down in the grass and die, just like he did.'' He laid his hands back on the towel in her lap, holding her attention with the passion in his eyes. ''I can also choose to live. I have an incurable disease, but it doesn't have to be fatal.''

She blinked back tears. ''I was so scared...when you went off with those other men.''

''I didn't stay with them long. I bought my own bottle, brought it here and drank until I couldn't smell burning horseflesh anymore.''

''Oh, Sage...''

''It's good that you saw...how it is with me. I can't be the perfect recovered alcoholic for you, Megan. There is no *recovered*. I'm recovering. I'm not the perfect anything.'' He offered a tentative smile. ''Just like the highway system in the summer, some part of me will always be under construction.''

''But four years is such a long time, and now—''

''It's still four years of sobriety. I didn't just erase them.''

''Why didn't you do something else?'' she asked urgently, as though what had happened could still be reversed if he were penitent enough. ''You said that when you still felt that—that need once in a while, you always went to a meeting or talked to someone.''

''I was busy watching everything I'd worked for burn to the ground,'' he reminded her dryly.

''Or you said you . . . prayed sometimes.''

''Yeah.'' He straightened his back and sighed. ''But you can't ask God to give you strength at the same time you're cussing Him out for turning His back on you.''

''So you believe in God.''

''Didn't I tell you I did?'' He looked at her as though he couldn't believe she'd forgotten something that important. ''I told you what I practice. There has to be a power stronger than mine. My ancestors used other words, but I'm comfortable with the word *God*. I sat up in that vision pit for days on end seeking His will for me. That's what a vision quest is. My own will is completely self-serving, and I'm powerless when it comes to alcohol.''

''Powerless?''

''That's right.'' He watched her digest that bombshell. Her hero had toppled. He couldn't help feeling a pang of regret.

She pushed back the chair and rose to her feet abruptly. "I can't think of you as being absolutely powerless over anything. Especially something you can choose not to consume."

"And that's what I have to do. But last night—"

"Last night was heartbreaking. I don't think last night counts. It would have taken a superhuman effort—what's so funny?"

"You are." He flopped back on the bed and rolled his head from side to side, chuckling. "You're so beautiful, it's funny. And what makes it even funnier is the fact that you're absolutely serious. God, how I'd love to let you make excuses for me, Megan, but I'm afraid last night *does* count." He lifted his head and caught her eye. "Unless you know of some way to rewind our lives back to yesterday and edit last night out."

"What happened yesterday can't be changed. What happened last night—"

He jackknifed into a sitting position again. "Is an old story. The Indian gets screwed, so he goes out and gets drunk. Which doesn't change the fact that he got screwed, and it limits his chances of making a comeback. So last night counts. If I don't deal with it, I'll be back where I was four years ago."

He stood up, facing her with more conviction than he'd had when she'd arrived. "I've decided I don't like getting screwed. I'm not letting them have the final say. It wasn't the barn they wanted, or the house. It was my sobriety." He turned a hard glance on the waste basket in the bathroom. "And they damn near got it, because I damn near started in again this morning.''

She followed his glance, then reached for his arm. ''Sage—''

He backed away. ''I'm not done, Megan. There's something else I don't like. I don't like it when you look at me like I'm some orphan kid who just got off the boat. What do you get out of that? Does that boost you up above the masses? Do you look at your dad that way, too?''

''My father?'' She stiffened, tilting her chin up as she informed him brusquely, ''My father has nothing to do with this. My father is not an alcoholic.''

''He's not? Then why do you want him to quit drinking?''

''I just think he drinks too much, that's all. I just...'' She crossed her arms over her chest, as was her custom. ''I don't feel sorry for you, Sage. I'm sorry about the fire, but I don't feel sorry for you. Okay?''

''Okay.'' They stared at one another through several silent moments. Finally he asked, ''So, without your sympathy, do I still have a job?''

''If you don't show up for work today, you get a warning,'' she told him. ''That's policy. If you have a medical excuse, of course, that's different, and you should have a doctor look at those hands.''

''And you should stop telling me what I *should* do. I'll be a little late, but I'll be there.''

''You can't come to work with hands that are all blistered like that.''

"Or a face that looks like hell?" He snatched his shirt off the bed. "Calling in sick is less embarrassing than walking in with an obvious hangover, right? If we cover it up carefully enough, maybe we can convince ourselves that I really didn't get drunk last night. Maybe we *can* edit it out."

She took a step closer to him. "Maybe we can stand around in this dump and argue about it all morning."

He moved closer, putting them almost nose to nose. "Maybe you can get out of here so I can get myself together and get to work."

"Fine." They watched each other ease off slowly. He took a step back and let her walk past him. She turned at the door, unable to resist trying for the last word. "I don't care what you do to your hands. And you're going to be late anyway." In a huff, she jerked at the door.

"I've got news for you, lady." She hesitated, and it amused him that she had to hear *his* parting shot. "So are you."

Chapter 12

Sage faced a steep uphill climb, and he found his first
handhold in his job. He made it through the first day
on a box of gauze bandaging and a tin of aspirin. That
evening he saw a doctor, who told him not to use his
hands for a couple of days. Since following such a
suggestion would have meant certain insanity, Sage
stocked up on gauze and antiseptic and decreed that
his hands should not be idle except during sleep. And
he worked. After work, with some help from friends
and neighbors, he hauled rubble from the ruins of his
buildings. After dark he met with the members of the
Medicine Wheel. No matter how small the circle, he
needed to be there, and the others knew it, so they
came.

Megan's attitude toward him was guarded. She
seemed to be afraid to laugh around him, as though

there had been a death in his family and his feelings might be fragile, like eggshells. They had always worked well together, and that hadn't changed. They let the road be their focus, the visible thread that bound them together. They discussed layers of compaction with such studied interest that their concern for the levels of their relationship wasn't apparent. When Sage felt her eyes on him, he held his breath and allowed the moment to pass. He was glad when his hands started healing. Once she'd discovered him washing them after they'd cracked open and begun to bleed, and he'd waited for her motherly comment. It hadn't come.

It seemed, then, that she was recovering, just as he was. Her recovery from her close call with a risky relationship would be healthy for both of them, he decided. It was good to see her, good to be near her so much of the time. By the time the job was over, maybe he would be content with a friendly parting, a congenial acknowledgment that working together had been a pleasure. By that time he hoped the need to touch her would have dulled and the exquisite memory of love's pleasures would actually feel like part of the past.

It bothered him to have to take time off from work to attend another liquor license hearing. This thing had gone on long enough, had played enough havoc in his life. It bothered him most of all because it meant bringing the issue up with Megan. She knew immediately why he needed an afternoon off. This time, when her blue eyes glistened with the soft light that said she was looking at Sage, the man, rather than Sage, the co-worker, he held her gaze. Despite the knot in his stomach, he knew it was time to talk.

"Pete tells me they've arrested someone in connection with the fire."

He laid his clipboard aside and leaned against the desk, resting his thigh along the edge. Megan took the cue and the space he'd left on the desk. "A guy named Gordon Brown. He was the guy who decided the barn burning was bring-your-own-bottle."

Megan shook her head slowly. "I thought for sure it was Floyd Taylor."

"I'm sure it was, but it looks like he used Brown. And so far Brown's not talking."

"And you didn't know this Gordon Brown?"

Sage turned his mouth down as he shook his head. "Never saw him before. Somebody who hired on for the summer with one of the local ranchers. I knew one of the guys he was with—good-time Lonnie. I don't think Lonnie knows anything."

"I wish they could get Taylor."

He chuckled. "A woman after my own heart." She glanced at him quickly, surprised, and he looked away. They endured an awkward moment of silence.

"How are you, Sage? I mean—" He turned his palms up to show her the healing. "I mean, how are you doing...otherwise."

He lifted his eyes slowly and let her see inside himself, if she cared to look. "Otherwise, I'm doing okay. I went back on Antabuse." Her puzzled look led him to explain. "It's a drug I took for about a year after I got out of treatment. If you drink any alcohol at all while you're taking it, you puke your guts out."

She winced. "That oughta cure you."

"Careful how you throw that word 'cure' around." Smiling, he lifted a forefinger. "Remember what I told you, there is no 'recovered,' only—"

"Only recovering. I know. And you are. I'm glad."

Her smiled warmed him inside. "I've started over before. It wasn't as tough this time. I had Medicine Wheel."

You had me, too, she thought. Only you didn't seem to notice. "What made you decide to quit the first time?" she asked. "Was it losing your wife?"

"The divorce was a long time coming. It was a relief to have it over—for both of us. But I wanted to be able to see the kids. I told her I'd fight for that much, at least. I told her—" He studied his hand and the healing that had already taken place, and he asked himself why it took so long to heal up inside.

"My daughter, Brenda...she was just six years old, but they grow up fast, you know? Anyway, the judge asked her how she'd feel about living with her dad. She told him she wanted to go with her mother." His voice became gruff, and he grimaced as he spoke. "She said she loved her dad, but she didn't want to be around him anymore because he was always drunk." His eyes were dewy with his pain, and the story seemed to echo, as though he'd forced it from the bottom of a well. "That didn't leave me with any delusions about fighting for my kids. Kids don't like watching their parents get drunk."

Megan's eyes widened as she wondered at the possibility. "So you made the decision to stop drinking for your daughter's sake."

"Hell, no." His chuckle was self-derisive. "I made the decision right then and there to drown the memory of that little face in a quart bottle. I ended up in treatment when one of my sisters committed me because I wasn't paying my lease."

"Oh," she managed quietly as she glanced away.

"Hey." He caught her chin with two gentle fingers and turned her face back to him. "If it's any consolation, you can't drown out the memory of disappointing someone you care about. It's still there when you sober up."

"So you start in again?"

He drew his hand back reluctantly. The contact, however small, had felt good to him. "That's the way an addiction works. Something has to break the cycle, and it's usually not the addict. In my case it was the wrath of a sister who wanted her lease check."

She caught his hand, touched her fingers to his palm and moved them slowly to the tips of his fingers. "Through it all, you worked so hard, even though your hands... When I saw how sore they were that time, I wanted to—"

"I know," he said in a raspy voice. "I know what you wanted to do."

"But you're healing yourself."

He shook his head. "I'm letting the healing take place." He sought understanding in her eyes. "So are you, Megan. By letting go. By not trying to claim that you have the power to *make* me get well."

"It's hard to believe that doing nothing is...is all I can do to help."

"You were pulling for me, weren't you?" His dark eyes glittered with his smile. "In your heart you were saying, 'God, I hope he makes it.'" She nodded and returned his smile. "See how that works? I need a lot of that."

Sage hoped a few of the people in the crowded council chambers were pulling for him as he took the witness' chair and adjusted the microphone. A clerk was distributing papers to the council members, and a man was offering coffee refills. Sage found that he'd missed a snap on his cuff, and he pressed it together. He'd hurriedly unrolled his shirt sleeves moments before, and now he wished he'd thought to wear a sport jacket. His tarnished image needed some polish.

He glanced over his shoulder to reassure himself that Regina and Bessie were still there. They were, but the fact barely registered as his eyes met Megan's. Why had she come? This was not to be his finest moment. He'd come forth with all the mortification of the prodigal son, and many of those present would take satisfaction in that. Why the hell did she have to be there? He took a deep breath and turned back to the microphone. The chairman gave him the signal to speak his piece.

"Mr. Chairman, I'm not going to repeat my position on this matter. You've heard it twice now. Mr. Taylor is asking for a temporary license, and I'm opposed to issuing him any license at all. Now, Mr. Taylor has already testified that denying his license would not prevent anyone from getting drunk, and he made a point to look at me when he said it." The room grew very still as Sage scanned the faces of the councilmen. "I had a relapse. It was nobody's responsibility but mine. The last time I sat in this chair, I was able to say it had been four years since I'd had a drink. Today I can only tell you it's been fourteen days. But those fourteen days were just as hard-won as the four years, and they tell me Medicine Wheel works if I work.

"So I'm working. I'm learning. I'm finding out that what tradition tells us about ourselves is true. We're a community. We're a circle of people whose lives are interwoven. The circle can be a source of strength for us. It can also be a weakness. When alcohol eats away at the fabric of our circle, our interdependency becomes a weakness. That's why I'm asking us to reject this application. I believe that as a people we need to say no to the way this man, Taylor, operates. Alcohol is taking too high a toll of us, and we need to get it out of our lives. For whatever reason, we're too susceptible. It destroys us.

"It was brought here and given to us a long time ago, and we had no more resistance to it than we had to measles. Then, later, they said, 'No, you guys better not drink that stuff. It's bad for you.' But by that time we were saying, 'Who the hell do you think you are? We'll drink it if we want to.' So we did. And we're suffering for it. And now it's time to say, 'We don't want to.' "

Megan listened to Sage's voice as it came through the microphone, filling the room with a rich, deep rumble. He slipped one hand beneath the table and wiped his palm on his thigh, and she rubbed her own together. They were sweating, too. No longer her image of an iron-willed hero, here was a man who was even more dear because he struggled with his imperfections and more courageous because he was not without fear.

"I know I said I didn't want to," Sage continued. "I said it loud and clear, and then I weakened. I know you won't forget that—I don't ask you to. I only ask you to accept me the way I am today—sober, and sincere in what I'm saying. Whatever you decide today, I'm going to keep saying it." He directed his gaze at Floyd Taylor and fought to control the anger he felt at the sight of the man. "I'm going to keep urging you to turn people like Floyd Taylor away. I've started rebuilding my barn. If it burns down again, I'll build it again. You can't stop me, Taylor. There's only one person who can destroy me, and that's *me*."

Taylor nearly tripped over himself trying to get to his feet. "If you're accusing me of anything, Parker, you damn well better have proof!"

"That's all I have to say, Mr. Chairman."

There was more testimony. Taylor had hired a glib attorney, and the proprietors of other liquor establishments objected to the precedent that might be set by turning one license down. In the end, a temporary license was granted, and Taylor was admonished to clean up his act. Megan stood aside as Medicine Wheel sympathizers gathered outside the front doors of the tribal office building, some shaking Sage's hand, some shaking their heads.

When Floyd Taylor and his associates appeared, heads turned and heated looks were exchanged. Taylor postured as he walked past Sage, throwing his shoulders back and looking around to be sure this was, indeed, the proper moment for a parting shot.

"You haven't changed, Parker. You come on down to Floyd's tonight. Your first one's on the hou—"

Sage's left fist hit Taylor's gut like a cannon ball. Over the man's breathless grunt, Sage muttered, "I *want* to change, Taylor." As Taylor's chin dipped, Sage caught it with a cracking right. "I've been working...damn hard at it." Taylor's big frame toppled into his friends' arms, while Sage's companions moved to restrain him, and to protect him from reprisal. He grinned broadly as he shook the cramp out of his right hand. "Guess I've still got a pretty bad temper."

Megan's heart pounded as she watched his friends spirit Sage away. She pressed her own right fist into her left hand and gave a secret smile.

After a solitary supper at the local café, she left town. The sun was August-evening gold hanging low in the western sky. She came to a junction and told herself that if she took the west fork, she would be squinting into the sun most of the way. The north fork would take her the long way around with less eye strain. She dismissed the added fact that she would pass Sage's place as she drove north.

His pickup was parked near the trailer. She surveyed the fire's aftermath as she negotiated the turn. The places where the house and barn had stood just weeks ago had been razed. Part of the corral had been saved, and the enclosure had been repaired with new lumber.

He stood on the small wooden platform that served as his front step. His white T-shirt was a beacon in the waning light.

"Checking up on me?" he asked quietly as she approached the steps. The pointed end of a wooden toothpick peeked out of the corner of his mouth.

Megan rejected "just passing by" as quickly as it came to mind and instead confessed, "I was hoping you'd be home."

"I haven't been here long." With a sweeping gesture he offered the wooden step. "Have a seat. It's cooler out here."

"You've done a lot of work already."

"I've about had my fill of the smell of charcoal." He sat beside her on the step and stretched his legs so that his boot heels rested on the ground. "I saw your pickup at the café. I thought about stopping, but decided I'd better get out of town before sunset." With a dry chuckle he leaned back on his arms and tipped his chin up. "I really blew it, didn't I?"

"Not at all," she protested. "You were eloquent."

"Eloquent?" He shifted the toothpick from one side of his mouth to the other as he raised a teasing eyebrow. "I never heard of an eloquent gut-buster before."

"Oh, that." She laughed and hugged her knees. "That part was magnificent."

"The lady's got a real mean streak."

"Only when somebody's got it coming, and I can't think of anyone who deserves it more than Floyd Taylor."

"That's probably the extent of the satisfaction I'm likely to get." He sat up and looked across the yard at the little corral as he draped his forearm over one bent knee. "Gordon Brown's white, so they can't try him in tribal court."

"It's a federal charge, isn't it?"

"Yeah."

"Isn't that better?"

"We'll see. Better than county court, I guess. Taylor's got too much local influence." He shrugged. "I'm not the court system's biggest fan." As he stared at the empty space where a barn would one day be resurrected, a slow, sinister smile spread across his face. "In this case, I'd be in favor of trial by fire. I've got plenty of charcoal. Turn them both on a spit, and if they get crisp, we pronounce them guilty as hell."

"Sage!"

"No, I was thinking salt, maybe Tabasco sauce." He watched her eyes brighten with laughter and considered how pretty she looked in pink. "Why did you come to the hearing today?" he asked quietly.

The laughter died, and she looked at him solemnly. "Not out of curiosity," she assured him. "I'm allowed to pull for you, right? That's all I was doing. Didn't you tell me there had to be witnesses? Somehow I think today's ordeal was more difficult than the Sun Dance must have been."

"Megan..." He sighed heavily, glanced away and then looked back at her. "The night of the fire, when I saw you drive up, I wanted to crawl into a hole. Not just because I was ashamed of the drinking, but I was...I was..." He groped for the words. Defeated? Beaten? He didn't like any of the words that came to mind. "A man feels... totally emasculated when a woman sees him pinned to the ground like that." God! That sounded worse than any of them.

"They've never pinned you to the ground." She put her hand on his shoulder. The warmth of his flesh under the soft cotton T-shirt stirred a matching warmth in her. "They take clumsy pot shots at you. As long as you keep coming back, they can't touch the man you are."

She could, he thought. She could touch the man he was, and he would never stop coming back. But she had to change, too. "Why did you come here tonight?"

She stiffened and drew her hand away. "Just to see you."

"To see if I was still sober?"

"I didn't think you'd..."

"I was disappointed over the decision, but I'm not going to get drunk over it. There are other ways." He leaned back on his elbow and admired the way the rosy sky behind her turned her into a softly shaded silhouette. "Regina's going to be able to open her store soon. If people are as tired of being jacked around by Taylor as they say they are, they'll take their business to Regina. If not—" He took the toothpick from the corner of his mouth and tossed it into the night. "If not, the hell with them."

"Really?"

"Really. You've gotta learn to recognize when enough's enough."

"You?" she asked. "Or the others?"

"Both." He offered a quick smile. "I'm not much of a host, am I? Would you like coffee?"

"If I can help you make it."

He laughed as he got to his feet. "Will you let *me* take care of *you* for once? Besides, it's made."

She took the hand he offered and followed him inside. "I'm not sure I understand this 'caretaker' thing. I'm far from a domestic, but I can make coffee." She closed the screen door behind her. "It just seemed polite to offer to help."

"It was." He pointed to a small overhead cupboard. "Get the cups. I hope you like it black, because I don't have anything to lighten it."

"Black is fine," she said. She set the cups down, and he poured from an aluminum percolator, which he'd left sitting over a low gas flame.

"Tell me about your dad," Sage suggested almost off-handedly. "Does he handle the checkbook, pay the bills?"

"Oh, no, he's no good with money. My mother takes care of that."

"Because she wants to?"

"She hates it." He nodded toward the door, and she swung the screen open again, assuming it bothered him to be cooped up inside. "He'd have it all messed up inside a week, that's all. I think if she could get him to stop..."

The conversation stalled as they settled on the steps again. Sage watched Megan hide her face behind her coffee cup. "Stop what?" he finally prodded.

She flashed wide, wary eyes. "I wasn't going to say 'drinking.'"

His patient smile was lopsided. "What else weren't you going to say?"

"I wasn't going to say that I don't ever have any thought of taking care of you...because...that wouldn't be entirely true."

"Fight the urge, Megan. It's destructive." The light from the kitchen illuminated the doubt in her eyes. He set his cup down and leaned closer, boring at her with his eyes. "It'll make you crazy," he told her. "It'll make you just as sick as I was when you saw me the morning after the fire. Sure, I needed a friend, but I didn't need a crutch. My disease is my problem, and if I do end up needing a crutch, it's got to be a wooden one, *not* a human one." He made an effort to inject a note of tenderness into his tone as he added, "It sounds to me like that's what your mother is, Megan. A human crutch."

Megan lowered her cup to the step slowly as her back stiffened. "That's not true, Sage. That's not even fair."

"It's not? Why not?"

"Because you don't even know them," she accused huskily.

"I know you." His voice was smooth, his tone sure, and that irritated her. "Alcoholism is a family disease, and I know one member of the family quite well. I see the symptoms."

"You're taking what I've confided in you, and you're blowing it out of—"

"You call him a 'problem drinker.' Why can't you call him an alcoholic?" He struggled to control the accusing edge in his voice, but it was there because of the way she sat up in front of him, so prim and perfect. "Why should your family be granted immunity? Huh? What other diseases *can't* you get? It's killing my people, and if you've got a vaccination against it, you damn well better—"

"I don't need any more of this." Megan pushed herself to her feet, tottering a bit as she reached her full height. "I have never said anything...unkind or..."

Sage set his cup down. "I'm not being unkind," he said evenly. "I just want to understand the real meaning behind the terms you use. Here we've got drunks. Winos. Off the reservation we've got 'problem drinkers.' I guess that sounds better. Does it look prettier? I mean, you haven't seen me when I'm really wasted, so it's probably hard to compare—"

She'd begun to tremble inside, and she wasn't sure why. She opened her mouth for a crisp goodbye, and it didn't come. Her throat burned, and she couldn't catch her breath. When he stood up gradually, she had the terrible feeling that he might hit her over the head, not with his hand, but with something worse—something that would hurt far more. She searched for some defense, and it came in a high-pitched retort.

"I've seen you with a hangover, and it looks the same on you as it does on anyone else. An old man's face, and sick to your stomach like a child!"

For a moment his boots were nailed to the step. He'd had no right, he told himself as he watched her turn and run. He'd pushed her too far. When he could move, he vaulted over the side of the step and caught up to her just as she reached her pickup.

"Megan!" He reached for her, but she jerked her arm away. "Look, I'm sorry. You're right, I don't know—"

"You know all about it, Sage. You're an expert!" The last word was nearly lost in her wild-eyed frenzy to get into the truck.

He felt as though, in one word, she'd thrown everything he'd confided in her back in his face. An expert! He grabbed the door. She tried to pull it shut, but her strength was no match for his. They eyed one another through the open window, black irises glittering, blue glinting back. Megan's chest heaved with each shallow breath as she waited for him to relinquish his hold.

"You can become an expert, too, Megan. You might as well. You're up to your eyebrows in it." His voice was soft and smoother than he'd thought he could manage. "Come to Medicine Wheel. They've listened to me for two solid weeks, and they're ready for somebody else. Or find a group that meets your needs. All you have to do is own up to the problem."

With that he shut the door and backed away. He watched her fumble with her keys, then go through the steps of putting the pickup in motion as though it were a new skill. She ground the forward gears, turned the headlights on as an afterthought and put thirty yards between them. The red brake lights came on. Sage gave her a few seconds, and when he was certain she was going no farther, he followed, stretching his long legs to cover the distance quickly. He found her slumped over the wheel, her shoulders shaking.

"Slide over," he said as he pulled the door open. She fought with the gear shift on the steering column until the pickup surrendered, choking out. Sage wanted to laugh at the muttered obscenity that sounded so unnatural on Megan's tongue, but he knew better. "It's okay," he said quietly. "Just let it go."

Let it go. He meant the pickup, but she heard more. The words were inviting, the concept incredible. It was a relief to let him take over, and when he took her in his arms, there was deliverance. She gave herself over to the tears and the awful quaking, trusting him to shield her while she did, indeed, let go. The solid flesh beneath his soft shirt offered support, and she leaned all her cares against it as she wept.

"He's not a bad man, Sage," she whispered. Whispering was all she could manage. Such a thing, even in the form of a denial, could not be said aloud.

"Am I a bad man?" he asked gently.

"No. Oh, no."

"I've done some bad things," he confessed. "I've had to recognize that and try to do something about it."

"He's my father." Her voice tripped over tears as the words tumbled out. "I can't not like...not love..."

"I know," he whispered. "It's okay, Megan."

"I can't help loving him," she choked. "I *do* love him, and it hurts because..."

"Because..."

"Because I love you too and I don't know what's wrong with me!" she shouted in a breathless rush.

"Nothing." His heart soared. He held her tighter and cherished the warmth of her tears against his neck. "There's nothing wrong with you, Megan."

"But I should know better!"

"Who says?" He coaxed her with kisses at her temple and in her hair. "It's okay to love me." He'd never been able to convince himself completely of that notion, but he wanted her to believe it. "I'm not a bad man." He poured small kisses over her face, praying she'd believe it, and she responded, straining to touch her lips to his face because it didn't matter whether she knew better. She loved him because she loved him because she loved him. . . .

His mouth was close to her ear, and his heart wedged itself in his throat. "Is it okay that I love you, too?"

"Yes."

"Will you stay with me tonight?"

"Yes."

"Sleep where I sleep?"

"Yes."

"Make me believe that I deserve to be loved?"

"If my love can do that for you."

He took her face in his hands and kissed the salty corners of her smile. "I believe it can."

He took her to the trailer, and for the first time since he'd lived there, he delighted in the walls' closeness. The little fan whirred in the dark as they undressed one another, maneuvering in a small warm space that reminded him of the sweat lodge. The earth's womb. Small and feminine, like the breasts he covered with

his hands. Persistent, like the nipples that formed hard
pebbles to tickle his palms. Round and smooth, like
the hips that housed the hearth of his heart's choosing.

The walls kept him close, as snug as a cocoon his
body had nearly outgrown. She slid her skin against
his, and he couldn't move away; it was as if some
wariness had grown in his mind.

The scent of musk filled her head and drove her to
touch him with boldly seeking hands. He was moist
satin skin over hard muscle everywhere she touched,
and he would fill her with power before they were
through. The thrill of anticipation rippled along the
insides of her thighs in a trail his fingertips blazed. She
spread her hands over his chest and made his nipples
tighten with her thumbs as she pressed him back upon
the bed.

"You deserve to be loved," she swore hotly.

Her hands worked magic.

"Oh, Megan . . ."

Her lips drove him mad.

"You're beautiful and caring, and I love you. All of
you."

Her tongue laved him to rigid readiness.

"You're too good," he said. "I want . . . too much
of you."

She took the device he clutched tightly in his hand
and slipped it over him with painstaking care, caring
for herself and for him and for the time they would
need to devote to one another. Then she sheathed him

within her body, letting him fill her, letting him know her, crying out when the joy could not be contained.

And Sage's tears touched her shoulder with the gentle beauty of a warm rain on rich earth, newly turned and springtime fertile.

Chapter 13

Megan's road lay like a shiny licorice whip over the small stretch of South Dakota prairie to which she would always lay some sentimental claim. It was mid-October, and though the evenings had grown cold, Indian Summer warmed the tawny hills through the waning afternoon hours. Megan's own little white Honda chased the broken yellow line from hollow to crest as she pushed past the speed limit to keep her date. She'd been invited to a picnic.

Sage was driving nails in his new subfloor when the white car turned into his long driveway. He'd been waiting for her, checking his watch every few minutes and keeping his hands busy with the hammer. The floor was nearly finished, as was the new pole barn. He hopped down from the plywood deck, untied the leather apron and stashed it with his hammer in his tool box just as Megan pulled up beside the pickup.

"Is this one of those working dates you're so famous for?" She smiled as he took her in his arms, but he kissed the smile away. She wound her arms around his neck and said hello his way.

"If I'm famous for them," he muttered between nibbles, "it's because you've been bragging them up."

"I can't help it," she murmured into his mouth. "I love to be envied."

"Me too. One of these days you can get dressed up, and I'll take you out to some big event. Make every guy in the place jealous of me." He lifted one corner of his mouth in a teasing smile. "Soon as the high school basketball season starts."

"Promises, promises."

"Aren't you going to say anything about the barn?"

He took her hand from the back of his neck and held it in his as she turned around. Her face lit up. "It's finished!"

"Almost. I've still got to get shingles and doors."

"But how did you . . . I mean, the last time I saw it, there were just . . ."

"Just a few poles. I know. A couple of the women from Medicine Wheel employed a time-honored Indian custom." He grinned, and golden sunlight glinted in the warmth of his autumn brown eyes. "They raffled off a couple of star quilts. Then they rounded up a bunch of people, and we had most of it done inside a day."

"That's wonderful, Sage." She slipped her arm around his waist and gave him a squeeze. "I think we should celebrate."

"I think so, too. I hope you didn't bring a bunch of food, like you usually do."

"Why not?"

"Because I told you I'd cook. Don't you trust me?"

The aroma of the freshly deep-fried bread she'd come to love in recent months filled the little trailer. It had been served at every function she'd attended on the Pine Ridge Reservation, and she'd attended quite a few. "I don't believe you actually made frybread," she said as he opened the door for her. His proud smile said that he'd just opened a package full of surprises. "Did you really?"

"You think I can't make anything but cold meat sandwiches? I learned a secret." He tossed her a conspiratorial wink. "Frozen bread dough."

"It works?"

"Pretty well." He handed her a stack of paper plates and a roll of paper towels. "You take the china." Then he reached for a cardboard box. "I'll take the picnic basket. Everything else is over there. You gonna be warm enough?" She glanced down at her fisherman knit sweater and nodded. "I'll take an extra blanket anyway. When that sun goes down, you really know it's fall."

He'd spread a star quilt over the grass amid the rows of cottonwoods. Its burst of orange, yellow and red gave the scattering of withered cottonwood leaves a taste of what autumn color should be. Megan giggled when she noted the plastic ice-cream pail at the corner of the quilt. Two green bottles of Perrier were planted in ice.

"I spared no expense for this occasion," he told her as he set the box next to the blanket.

"I did bring a little dessert."

"Did you, now." After taking the plates from her first, he pulled her down beside him and cupped his hands over her breasts. "A little dessert? I always love your *little* desserts."

"You may not get any if you say 'little' one more time," she said imperiously, but she gave him a small kiss, which held out some promise.

"Keep that up and we'll have cold frybread."

She settled on the blanket and watched him open the first bottle. "Frybread and Perrier make a very interesting combination."

"Oh, it gets better," he promised as he poured a small amount of the sparkling water into a plastic glass. "How do Indian tacos and Perrier strike you?"

"Sounds heavenly. I won't have to worry about being little much longer with this kind of feasting." She lifted the plastic glass toward the setting sun and smiled as the tiny bubbles became glinting jewels. "Excellent clarity."

"Well, hell, it's French. What can I say?"

She swirled, sniffed and sipped. "Tangy. It has a life of its own. I believe you can actually taste the granite from the spring."

Sage poured himself some and tossed it down. "Not much kick to it," he judged. "Let's try the tacos."

The flat pieces of frybread were piled high with hot, spicy hamburger and fresh salad. Megan held the plate just inches from her mouth, which she stretched wide to accommodate the layers of food. The taste of chili and Cheddar cheese complemented the warm, chewy bread. Spicy red juice dribbled down her chin, and Sage tossed her the roll of paper towels. When the same thing happened to him, she tossed it back. The messiness of the concoction was part of its appeal.

It was impossible to talk with their mouths full of shredded lettuce and heavy bread, but when they were down to the Perrier and the prospect of dessert, Sage announced that he'd sold his calves and gotten a good price. He'd bought seven bred heifers, which brought his herd up to twenty-one.

"I kept one steer calf," he told her. "I'll feed him over the winter and donate him for the dinner when Regina has her giveaway next summer."

"How's her store doing?"

"She's taking a big cut out of Taylor's business, *and*—" He raised one eyebrow in delight. "Old Floyd isn't selling as much booze these days as he'd like to."

It had been slow in coming, but Sage's victory was beginning to taste sweet. Gordon Brown had been indicted on charges of arson, and he was awaiting trial in federal court. There was still hope that he might implicate Taylor.

"The Medicine Wheel program is growing, isn't it?"

"They've got a strong group in Pine Ridge, and we're running a meeting just about every night now in Red Calf."

She held her cup out for more water. "Do you think I'd be welcome, sort of. . . on a regular basis?"

He gave her a puzzled look. "Sure, you're always welcome, but that's a long way to drive from Pierre. I thought you'd found a group there that you liked."

"I did." She studied her glass. She hadn't told him, because she didn't know how he'd react. She suspected the distance between them was a kind of safety valve for him. "I'm moving," she announced finally.

"Moving," he repeated slowly. "Moving... here?"

"I'm going to work for Pete Petersen at the roads department in Pine Ridge."

"You didn't tell me you were applying for a BIA job."

She made herself look up. "I applied last summer. I didn't know whether I'd get it, and when it was offered, I didn't know whether to take it. I talked to Pete and Bob Krueger, and then I gave it a lot of thought." The look in his eyes didn't change. He was disturbed. "It's a good opportunity for me. Pete'll retire in a couple of years, and if I like the job and I'm what they need, I might..."

"I don't understand why you didn't tell me."

She sighed. "I didn't tell you because...I needed to look at the job...apart from us. It had to be good for me, for my career."

"It does bring you...more within reach, though."

"It does," she said quietly.

"I don't know about you, but I like that idea." A broad smile slid across his face and touched his eyes. He lifted his glass. "In fact, I'll drink to it."

When the glasses were drained, he pulled a letter from his shirt pocket. "Here's something else I've got to celebrate. It's from Brenda."

"Your daughter? She finally answered your letters?"

He nodded as he pulled the lined notebook paper from its envelope. "You can read it. It's not like she's dying to see me or anything, but she remembers me, and her mom said it was okay to write to me if she wanted to.'' His eyes glistened as he handed Megan the letter. "She wanted to.''

Two small school pictures slipped out when she unfolded the paper. There was a dark-haired boy whose new permanent teeth were still too large for his little-boy face and a dark-eyed girl who, in a few short years, would be a lovely young woman. Megan knew how much older they must have looked to Sage, and her chest grew tight at the thought of all he'd missed.

"They look so much like you," she said.

"You think so? I . . . I kinda thought so, too."

Megan unfolded the letter and read the message written in the carefully rounded hand of a twelve-year-old. "She says she remembers riding double with you, and she remembers how you used to call her 'Shorty.' And—" She looked up as she folded the letter and tucked it back in the envelope. His eyes were filled with a bitter-sweet mixture of emotion. "She's so glad you've stopped drinking.''

"I told her I was working hard at it. I didn't tell her—"

"You told her the truth, Sage." She reached for him, putting her arms around his neck. "I need to hold you," she whispered, pressing her palm over his soft sweatshirt.

"I need to hold you, too." He pulled her into his lap and crushed her to him. Their needs had nothing to do with pity. There was pain to be acknowledged and joy to be shared, but there was no bid for sympathy and no caretaking.

"I went to see my father," she told him.

"How did it go?"

"I just told him that I was participating in a group for adult children of alcoholics."

"What did he say?"

She leaned back, holding his head in her hands. "He said he'd never heard of such a thing, and my mother said that groups were the in thing these days. I think he was hurt. I think she was a little angry."

"You're not doing it for him," he reminded her.

"I'm doing it for me."

She was learning. He grinned as he sneaked his hands beneath her sweater. "That's right. Now, how about doing something for me?"

"I suppose you want dessert."

"Right again." He lowered her back against the cotton quilt, and she heard the crackle of the bed of leaves beneath it.

"I really did bring some, you know."

He pushed her sweater out of the way and nuzzled the ivory satin that covered her ivory skin. Both soft. Both powder scented. "I know you did." He nudged at the satin with his nose. "Little tart."

"I warned you about—"

"Mmm, two little tarts." He sucked at her through the satin.

She took a deep breath. "That word *little*."

"Two for me," he muttered as he moved to taste the second one. "And none for you."

"I brought..." He released the clasp between her breasts, and she sighed. "...something...that probably isn't very..."

"I'm stealing these tarts," he whispered, "with these sweet little round..."

He unbuttoned her jeans and inched the zipper down while he feasted. "...very good..." Megan breathed. She buried her fingers in his thick hair for support as her thighs went slack. "Oh, Sage, that feels...very, very...good."

"You like that?"

"Mmmm."

"You hungry?"

"Mmmmmmmm."

"How about an éclair?"

Her hand crept under his sweatshirt and over his belly, and he sucked his breath in when it reached the waistband of his jeans. "Do you have one for me?" she whispered hotly.

"Mmm-hmmm. Somewhere."

"Let me find it."

The sky ran riot with bright white stars, and a pumpkin-colored harvest moon hung low above the jagged horizon. Wrapped together in a blanket and in one another's arms, they shared dreams and intimate touches and listened to the last of summer's leaves answer the night breeze with a dry rustle.

"Do you think we'll ever build another road together?" Megan asked.

"I think I'm supposed to build roads," he said absently, enjoying the feel of the soft down on the back of her neck as he stroked her. "All kinds of roads."

"If I did a vision quest, do you think I'd find out what I'm supposed to do?"

He dipped his chin and feathered his lips across her forehead, wondering what she dreamed about now when she closed her eyes. "What if you did one and it told you to go back to Pierre and find some guy who's already got his act together? Then what?"

"How many times did you say you went back to the vision pit?"

"Three."

"Then I'd try again." She levered herself up on one arm and traced the lines across his brow with her thumb. "I've learned a lesson from you, Sage Parker." Care lines, she thought. She cherished each one. "You're only beaten when you stop trying."

"I love you."

"And I love you."

* * * * *

If you enjoyed this book, look for SOMEDAY SOON, Kathleen Eagle's first Silhouette Special Edition, available again this November—only from Silhouette Classics.

Author's Note

The town of Red Calf and the Medicine Wheel program are fictitious. The concept for Medicine Wheel, however, was inspired by the story of Alkalai Lake, a community of the Shuswap people in British Columbia. There the courageous decision of one woman led to recovery for herself, her husband and, eventually, almost the entire community. Native American people in a number of North and South Dakota communities are designing their own recovery programs, revitalizing an ancient heritage of spirituality as they attack the problem of alcoholism with new self-confidence and a tradition of wisdom as old as the rolling hills of the Dakotas.

TALES OF THE RISING MOON
A Desire trilogy by Joyce Thies

MOON OF THE RAVEN—June (#432)
Conlan Fox was part American Indian and as tough as the Montana land he rode, but it took fragile yet strong-willed Kerry Armstrong to make his dreams come true.

REACH FOR THE MOON—August (#444)
It would take a heart of stone for Steven Armstrong to evict the woman and children living on his land. But when Steven saw Samantha, eviction was the last thing on his mind!

GYPSY MOON—October (#456)
Robert Armstrong met Serena when he returned to his ancestral estate in Connecticut. Their fiery temperaments clashed from the start, but despite himself, Rob was falling under the Gypsy's spell.

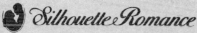

Silhouette Romance

A Trilogy by Diana Palmer

Bestselling Diana Palmer has rustled up three rugged heroes in a trilogy sure to lasso your heart! The titles of the books are your introduction to these unforgettable men:

CALHOUN

In June, you met Calhoun Ballenger. He wanted to protect Abby Clark from the world, but could he protect her from himself?

JUSTIN

In August, Calhoun's brother, Justin—the strong, silent type—had a second chance with the woman of his dreams, Shelby Jacobs.

TYLER

October's long, tall Texan is Shelby's virile brother, Tyler, who teaches shy Nell Regan to trust her instincts—especially when they lead her into his arms!

Don't miss TYLER, the last of three gripping stories from Silhouette Romance!

Silhouette Intimate Moments

COMING NEXT MONTH

#261 SMOKE SCREEN—Emilie Richards

Paige Duvall had come to Waimauri, New Zealand, to forget a painful past, not embark upon a future. But then she met handsome sheep farmer Adam Tomoana, a man who held the secret to her heritage, and quite possibly her heart.

#262 FLOWER OF THE DESERT—Barbara Faith

Strong-willed Princeton coed Jasmine Hasir had always been able to take care of herself. But that was before she was kidnapped by a nomadic horseman in the lawless Sahara sands. Then only the power of love—and Raj Hajad—would be able to rescue her.

#263 CROSSCURRENTS—Linda Turner

Mitch Flannery had never trusted anyone; his work in the Secret Service had taught him that. But his prime suspect, Serenity Jones, had too much integrity to be a criminal. And when she became a killer's prime target, Mitch had to learn a new lesson. Only his faith could give them a future—together.

#264 THE NAME OF THE GAME—Nora Roberts

Television game show producer Johanna Patterson knew the larger-than-life people of show business were just that: unreal. But she soon realized that actor/contestant Sam Weaver wasn't playing a game. He *really* was determined to gain her trust—and win her love.

ATTRACTIVE, SPACE SAVING BOOK RACK

Display your most prized novels on this handsome and sturdy book rack. The hand-rubbed walnut finish will blend into your library decor with quiet elegance, providing a practical organizer for your favorite hard-or soft-covered books.

Only $9.95

Approximately 16" x 8" when assembled

Assembles in seconds!

To order, rush your name, address and zip code, along with a check or money order for $10.70* ($9.95 plus 75¢ postage and handling) payable to *Silhouette Books.*

Silhouette Books
Book Rack Offer
901 Fuhrmann Blvd.
P.O. Box 1396
Buffalo, NY 14269-1396

Offer not available in Canada.

BKR-2A

*New York and Iowa residents add appropriate sales tax.

In October
Silhouette Special Edition
becomes
more special than ever
as it premieres
its sophisticated new cover!

Look for six soul-satisfying novels
every month . . . from
Silhouette Special Edition